POLLY WATCHED

HORROR as the British charged the American lines—and reeled back from the storm of musket fire. The blast echoed across the bay to where she stood. **Ethan's there,** she thought **—can he live through that?**

The British lines re-formed and charged again. Men fell—but the redcoats pressed on and broke the Colonial line. The battle of Bunker Hill was over . . .

. . . and Polly began her search of the battlefield for the man she loved. When she found him, he was all right—only lightly wounded. And, held tightly in Ethan's arms, she knew that through the long war to come, she would follow him and share the peril—

for without Ethan,
her life would be over.

Bride of Liberty

Frank Yerby

PYRAMID BOOKS • NEW YORK

BRIDE OF LIBERTY

A.PYRAMID.BOOK—published by arrangement with The William Morris
        Agency

PRINTING HISTORY—Doubleday edition published September 1954
        Pyramid edition published June 1964

With the exception of actual historical personages
identified as such, the characters are entirely the
product of the author's imagination and have no
relation to any person or event in real life.

Library of Congress Catalog Card Number 54-7595

Copyright, 1954, by Frank Yerby   All Rights Reserved

Printed in the United States of America

PYRAMID BOOKS are published by Pyramid Publications, Inc.,
444 Madison Avenue, New York, N.Y. 10022, U.S.A.

BRIDE OF LIBERTY

"But, Mama," Polly Knowles said, "why must we do this? Nobody else sprinkles sand on the parlor floor. And they certainly don't sweep it into curliques, and then lock up the room . . ."

Gertrude Knowles looked at her younger daughter.

"Ach, child," she said gently, "you will never understand . . ." When she said will, it sounded like "vill," and she pronounced never, "nefer." For Gertrude Knowles had been born Gertrude van Rijn, and she ran her house the way she did because the Dutch had always done things that way.

"I know, I know!" Polly burst out, "Grandpapa van Rijn was a patroon, and before him, his father was, too. But Mama, this is 1774, not ancient times. And I'm not Dutch; I'm English! I hate this house! Why can't we live in a Georgian house of red brick like everybody else? When I come home and see all those yellow and pink and blue and red bricks in patterns in our walls, I could just die, Mama—really I could!"

Gertrude stopped her careful tracing in the clean white sand on the parlor floor.

"I think you will not die," she said, "but I think if you do not learn better manners, you will hurt a little. Go outside in the air. I will finish. Ach, Gott, but to have two daughters and no sons is a trying thing! Fifteen she is, and already with the silly vapors!"

"I'm sorry, Mama," Polly said. But she put down her broom made of rushes and skipped down the hall. She was glad to be free of the boring business of arranging the parlor.

As she came out on the stoop, she could hear her sister Kathy playing the spinet inside the sitting room. The notes made a tinkling little run, quavering on the air. There isn't any justice in this world, Polly thought bitterly. Why should Kathy have inherited all the Van Rijn beauty, and all the Knowles' accomplishments?

Pretty Kathy Knowles, people always said. Kathy had silvery-blond hair, and eyes the color of violets, and a pink mouth that everybody wanted to kiss. She had a good figure, too, that required very little pulling at her stays, and that men's eyes followed with the kind of interest in them that they never had when they looked at Polly.

I am as straight as a stick, Polly wailed. My nose turns up—and it's got freckles on it. And nobody—not Ethan or anybody else—ever said my eyes were like flowers. They're the color of old rusty pennies and my hair—Susie, my mare, has a prettier mane!

In the sitting room, Kathy laughed suddenly, her clear soprano rising above the music. Two or three other voices joined in her laughter. Deep-toned voices, masculine and rich.

How could she? Polly raged. If I had Ethan, I'd never look at another man . . .

But you don't have Ethan, she told herself. He's going to marry Kathy. Papa has approved the match. It's going to take place on the fifteenth of September —next month. And Kathy is your sister . . .

It was, she realized suddenly, a little like saying that she was going to die on the fifteenth of September. But she wasn't. She knew that. She was going to have to live on, knowing . . .

The little landau came around the side of the house. Michael was driving, and her mother sat in the back seat, holding a little umbrella.

"I go to your Aunt Heide's," Gertrude said. "Tell Papa . . ."

"Yes, Mama," Polly answered her listlessly, and promptly forgot all about it. She just sat there on the stoop of her father's house on William Street, near Wall, almost in the exact center of New York City in this year of Our Lord, 1774, and concentrated upon being unhappy.

Outside, in the locust trees that shaded William Street, the katydids started chirping. That she could hear them made Polly notice how quiet things had become in the parlor. They're probably playing some disgusting old kissing game, she thought. But in the next instant, she admitted to herself that if she only could play kissing games with Ethan, she wouldn't find them disgusting at all. Polly Knowles was nothing if not honest.

She could hear the lowing of the cows now. It sounded far off and faint, like deep bells plunged into the wind. That meant that old Ebenezer, their Negro man, was bringing them back from the pastures west of Broadway. Polly could guess the time from that. In a few minutes, her father, Patrick Knowles, would come walking up the street from his offices on Maiden Lane, three blocks away.

I'm going to talk it over with Papa, she thought.

I'm going to say: "Papa, what does a girl do when she's in love with a man who . . ."

But she wouldn't. Just to think of asking her father such a thing paralyzed her with fear. That was the bad thing. She had no one to talk to. There wasn't a living soul in all New York who'd listen.

Mama would, Polly thought. But then she'd end up by giving me sulphur and molasses to cure me of my silly vapors. That's her cure for everything—even love. I wonder if she ever felt toward Papa the way I feel about Ethan? You never can tell about the Dutch. They hide their feelings so well . . .

Funny Papa isn't home yet. Guess he stopped in the tavern to have some applejack with Mr. Page. Thank goodness they haven't gone on quarreling. It wouldn't do to have bad feelings between in-laws. . . .

They were laughing again inside the sitting room, and she heard two of the boys saying good-by to Kathy. From their voices, Polly knew that they were the Gilmore twins, George and Henry. They came out of the house now, and sauntered off down the street, scarcely bothering to salute Polly at all.

Boys! Polly frowned. And the one that was left, that Millard Whitney—why he was the worst of them all.

I hate him! Polly thought. I'd much rather he were like the rest, yapping at Kathy's heels. But not Millard. He has to pay court to Kathy when Ethan's not around; then when Ethan comes he's always trying to kiss me . . . I hate . . .

She stopped short before she even finished the thought. The little open carriage that drew up before the gate had come from the direction of Broadway, so she hadn't seen it. But now she saw it, and she had trouble with her breath. For the life of her she couldn't move, so she just sat there while Ethan Page waved to her gaily and then climbed down and tied the two horses to the hitching rail.

He came walking toward her now, and she knew she had to get up. She had to stand up and offer him her hand and curtsy. She had to say something to him. But what did one say? What were the words?

"Ethan—my Ethan." Say that. Say: "Your eyes are so very blue. And they laugh all the time. How came you by such eyes, my Ethan? What are they doing in a face as brown as any Indian's, under hair that even a night sky without a single star couldn't match?"

What she actually said was: "Why, Ethan! No wig?"

It was, she knew at once, an idiotic thing to say. But Ethan's mouth widened in his lean face, and there were crinkles at the corners of his eyes.

"I've moss enough of my own growing," he laughed. "I don't need to borrow another man's . . ."

"You—you've changed," Polly rushed on helplessly. "Your clothes—you used to dress so fine!"

Ethan glanced down at his plain brown coat without a trace of braid or gold thread or any kind of embroidery. His vest was fawn-colored, his knee pants the same color as his coat. Even his shoes were plain, with simple buckles of silver. The three-cornered hat under his arm was brown too, and equally innocent of ornament. Yet the Pages were even richer than the Knowles, and Polly had seen Ethan many times in a habit à la Française, of sky-blue silk, embroidered all over with silver, and a white cadogan wig which alone had cost enough to pay a poor man's debts for a year.

Yet his blue eyes, when he looked at his simple garb, held a light of quiet pride.

"In Philadelphia," he said quietly, "I met a man called Benjamin Franklin. He dresses like this. And he wears his own hair—what there's left of it. The first time I talked with him, I noticed that he was looking at my clothes—with pity. And when I'd talked with him a few more times, I knew why . . ."

"Why, Ethan?" Polly whispered.

"Because it's what's inside a man's head and heart that counts—not what he drapes over his hide. We're breeding a new man in these so-called Colonies, Polly. A new breed on earth, maybe—a Republican. And all the fripperies and foppery of artificial distinction like birth and privilege have to go. They disgrace the dignity of the kind of men we'll have to be. . . ."

Polly heard what he said, but she didn't understand him. She never listened to Ethan with her mind anyhow. She didn't need to. Whatever Ethan said or thought was right to her without any need for comprehension. Her heart accepted it without any carping criticism from her usually quite analytical brain.

"What were you doing in Philadelphia, Ethan?" she asked, but he grinned at her.

"Tell you later," he said. "Where's Kathy?"

Polly's arm came up like the arm of a marionette pulled by invisible strings.

"In there," she said, and pointed. Her voice was so low that Ethan didn't hear her words at all. He merely saw the gesture.

"Thank you, my dear," he said, and gave her cheek an affectionate pinch. Then he opened the door and entered the house.

I won't cry! Polly stormed. I won't. But she did. She had barely time to dash the tears from her eyes with the back of her hand when Ethan came out again with Kathy on his arm, and Millard Whitney trailing at their heels for all the world like a fat, pink poodle.

"Come on," Ethan said. "We're going for a ride. Millard will keep you company." He bent close to her ear. "Over DeVoor's Mill Stream," he whispered. "Some fun, eh, Polly?"[1]

"No!" Polly cried, and stamped her foot. "I wouldn't ride over Kissing Bridge with that fat idiot if he were the last boy on earth! And if you ever"—she turned upon Millard—"try to kiss me again, I'll—I'll scratch out both your eyes!" Then she whirled and fled into the house, leaving a trail of quite audible sobs behind her.

Ethan stared at Kathy.

"Now what on earth has got into her?" he said.

Kathy tossed her head so that the late afternoon sunlight tangled in the blond hair she had gotten from her Dutch ancestors.

"Don't you know?" she said.

"No," Ethan said.

"Then far be it from me to tell you. My little sister is getting to be far too pretty even with that plain brown hair and eyes . . ."

Ethan looked at Kathy gravely.

"Yes," he said, "Polly is pretty." Then the ghost of a smile began to play about the corners of his wide mouth. "But there's one slight difference between you . . ."

[1]Now Fifty-second Street and Second Avenue. Every woman who crossed Kissing Bridge over that now long since filled in creek, regardless of her marital status or lack of it, was kissed by her escort.

"And what is that?" Kathy asked.

"She's pretty. You—you're beautiful."

Kathy dropped him a half-mocking curtsy.

"Thank you, kind sir!" she laughed. Then she took his arm and the two of them went down the steps and left poor Millard standing there staring after them.

He thought for a moment of going back into the house to seek out Polly. But he remembered the expression on her face when she had threatened to blind him. So he clapped his tricorne down on the untidy white wig that looked for all the world like a mass of gray-white hay and went on down the steps and out into the street.

Inside the house, Polly was lying across her bed, crying. That didn't last very long, for Polly was not the type to give in to her emotions over any length of time. Ten minutes after Ethan and Kathy had driven away, Polly got up and washed her face in cold water and came back downstairs.

She went and sat in her father's study, which she was forbidden to do. But in her present mood she had to do something out of the ordinary. She sat there and glared at the shrunken head of an Indian that some of her father's sailors had brought him back from Brazil.

I wish I'd die, she thought bitterly, then I'd write in my will that they'd have to shrink my head like that and send it to Eth and Kathy for a wedding present!

She took a morbid delight in imagining the expressions on their faces when they opened the box and drew out her head. The way she thought they'd look was so funny that she had to laugh. After that she felt better, so she wandered through the house looking at the treasures that her father had accumulated during thirty years as an importer.

There were the colored fabrics from Java, called "batiks," the curiously carved little Chinese figures, the Japanese screen, with dragons and peacocks painted on it, the bamboo chair from Jamaica. Polly examined them all, but they didn't impress her very much. What she liked best were the thin cups, saucers, and plates of china, painted with flowers, hunting scenes, racing scenes, so fine and delicate that her mother spoke of them as paper-shell china and hung them on the wall as ornaments, never putting them to use.

Ordinarily, Polly and the rest of the Knowles ate out of pewter dishes—made for the most part by the great foundry of Daniel Page, Ethan's father. Daniel was a great artist in pewter and silver, and Ethan had inherited much of his skill. Polly dimly sensed that the things the Pages made were lovely. But she was to be an old woman, and many times a grandmother, before she learned just how beautiful they were.

She touched them now out of love and tenderness, but they made her want to cry again. So she put them down in some haste, especially since she heard her father's footsteps sounding through the house.

"Gertie!" Patrick roared. "Gertie, my love—where in the name of heaven are you?"

His tone startled Polly. He sounded like a man who had been mortally wounded. She ran out of the library, past the closed door of the parlor that her mother always kept locked so that no one could disturb the white sand, swept into curious curlicues that she covered the floor with. Only important guests ever saw the inside of that room.

"Yes, Papa?" she said as she stopped at the door of his study.

"Your mother," Patrick groaned. "Where's your mother?"

"Gone to Aunt Heide's. Can I help you, Papa? You look downright ill . . ."

"I am, child. Go and make your old father a flip, right away."

Polly stood there a moment longer, staring at her father as he punched the tobacco into one of his long-stemmed clay pipes with his thumb, spilling most of it in the process. Then he fumbled with his fire maker, a little flintlock pistol with no barrel, but with a small tinderbox under the flintlock to catch the sparks. Finally he succeeded in lifting a smoldering bit of lint from under the tinderbox and putting it in the bowl of his pipe. Then he puffed away noisily.

"Off with you, girl!" he roared. "I must have a hot flip!"

Polly skipped into the kitchen, where there was always a roaring fire. Why anyone wanted a hot flip in August was more than she could see. But she put the long poker, called a loggerhead, into the fire to heat. Taking down a pewter pitcher, she filled it two thirds full of strong beer. Then she added sugar until the beer was sweet and filled the pitcher up to the brim with rum. Opening the stove, she looked at the loggerhead. It wasn't hot enough, so she waited. When it was red hot, she drew it out and stirred the mixture with it until it boiled.

She tasted it and made a face. How anyone could

drink a hot flip was more than she could see. And in the summertime, too! Something must have upset Papa terribly.

She brought this formidable concoction back to the library and watched her father as he downed it almost at a gulp, hot as it was.

The sweat burst out on his red face. He eyed her narrowly.

"Where's your sister?" he growled.

Polly hesitated. Then it occurred to her that since Kathy and Ethan were officially engaged, no harm could come of telling the truth.

"Out riding with Ethan," she said.

"Damme!" Patrick exploded. "Well, 'twas my own fault. I always knew that young gamecock was of uncertain temper. But Dan'l! That sinks me. I'll be blessed if I ever thought . . ."

"If you ever thought what, Papa?" Polly prodded.

"Never you mind, missy. 'Tis no concern of yours. One thing, though. When that precious pair returns, have both of them shown into my study at once."

"Yes, Papa," Polly said dutifully, but a wild hope stirred at her heart. If Ethan had done something that Papa didn't approve of, the engagement would be ended at once. This was no marriage of convenience. The Knowles and the Pages were almost equal as far as wealth was concerned. Patrick Knowles didn't need to worry overmuch as to the state of a prospective son-in-law's fortune. Polly's hope was based upon a long-term view of things. As fickle as Kathy was, she'd soon turn to another suitor. And when she was married and out of the way . . .

Polly hugged herself, just thinking of it. Then she

looked at her father. Papa is so stern, she thought. But he's just, according to his lights. I guess I'm the only one who really knows him. Not even Mama understands him as I do. He believes in things so hard, and he's stricter with himself than with anyone else. He's just got to be just—even when it hurts. I think he's really kind, and is ashamed of his kindness. He sort of regards it as weakness. If only he could learn to be a little merciful, the way he truly longs to be. . . .

She skipped to the front door to wait. She didn't have to wait long. Already Tim O'Mallory, their Irish boy, was lighting the lantern in front of the house. And no unchaperoned couple would dare stay out long after dark, even if they were engaged. There was still enough daylight to see by when the little carriage drew up to the door. Watching the gallantry with which Ethan helped Kathy down from the carriage, Polly felt fishhooks inside her body. Fishhooks and brambles and knives.

They came up on the stoop. Ethan was getting ready to kiss Kathy good night. Polly had to stop that.

"Papa wants to see you," she blurted. "Both of you—in his study—right away!"

Ethan frowned. Then his face relaxed.

"Thanks, Polly," he said.

Polly held the door open for them. After they had passed, she walked a couple of steps behind them. That way she was able to get into the study with them. She stopped at once, standing in the deep shadow. Patrick Knowles had only one candle lit, so much of the study lay in darkness. A bottle of arrack stood at his elbow, already three quarters empty. Polly shivered. She knew what a villainous temper arrack always put her father into. It was distilled from rice and molasses, and was almost as bad as the gin the slaves and bonded servants drank. Like all aristocrats, Patrick scorned gin. The lower classes called it "Strip and Go Naked." It sometimes made them do that, too—even in the dead of winter. But arrack was as bad. It was her father's fighting drink.

Patrick turned his small brown eyes up at Ethan's face. They were already streaked and bloodshot. They glittered in the light of the candle.

"Young man," he said grimly, "are you, too, a traitor to our King?"

Ethan stared at him.

"What do you mean, sir?" he asked quietly.

"You know right well what I mean. This morning I had the melancholy intelligence that your father— a man of sense and parts, whom I've always been proud to call friend . . ."

"Thank you for that, sir," Ethan said.

"Don't interrupt! As I was saying, I was told this morning that your father is to be a delegate to that so-called Continental Congress which will meet next month in Philadelphia. Is that true?"

Ethan smiled.

"It is, sir," he said, "I'm proud to say."

Patrick Knowles stood up, his bulk almost filling the study. He was much bigger than Ethan—taller and heavier.

"Proud!" he said in a hoarse whisper. "So you share your father's sentiments, eh?"

"I go with him, sir, as his alternate," Ethan said.

"Then there is nothing further that need be said,"

Patrick got out. "Kathy, you will give the young man back his ring."

"Oh, Papa!" Kathy wailed.

"Do as I say!" Patrick thundered.

Polly looked at her sister. If it were I, she thought, I'd refuse. I'd defy Father even if he caned me within an inch of my life. I'd die in my tracks before I'd give Ethan up. But you aren't like me, are you, Kathy?

Then she stood there smiling, as Kathy drew off the plain circle of gold and handed it to Ethan with trembling fingers.

Ethan let it rest in the palm of his hand. He looked at it a long time, and his face was grave. Then very slowly he turned his hand over and let it fall to the floor.

"I don't want it," he said quietly. "It has been dishonored, I think—by bigotry, and by cowardice. Good night to you, sir. And to you, Mistress Knowles." Then he bowed and went out the door.

Polly raced after him.

"Eth!" she called.

He turned to her.

"Yes, Polly?" he said.

"I—I'm with you!" she said breathlessly. "If you think the Congress is right, then it is right! I just know it!"

Ethan smiled down at her.

"Thank you for that, little Polly," he said.

Polly stamped her foot so hard that it hurt through the sole of her shoe.

"Don't call me little Polly," she said angrily. "I'm a woman grown, and I know my own mind!"

Ethan laughed, in spite of his heavy heart.

"You grown?" he chuckled. "Now I'll tell one!"

It was then that Polly was moved to desperate measures. She went up on tiptoe and locked both her arms about his neck. Then she kissed his mouth, hard.

Ethan stood there a long time after she had turned him loose and fled up the stairs to her room. He was a handsome lad. He had kissed and been kissed by many a maid. But never before quite so thoroughly. Never in all his life. He was sure of that.

I'll be blessed, he thought. You know—she's right at that!

He put his hat on his head and marched out of the house like a soldier. Over the Hudson, great clouds had piled up, purple and deep, blotting out the stars. As he unhitched his horses, heat lightning flared, and afterward there was the slow, belly-deep roll of thunder. To Ethan's ears, it sounded like guns.

As he climbed into the driver's seat, he shivered a little. There was something prophetic in that sound.

CHAPTER 2

Polly lay flat on her stomach with her head propped up on her two hands. It was easy for her to lie like that because the hoops in her skirt didn't go all the way around her, but merely stuck out on her two sides. Seen from the front, it made the lower half of her look very broad, but from the side she was very narrow and flat, having only her own colt-like slenderness to support her garments.

She was reading a book that Ethan had brought her back from Philadelphia. The light that came through the many diamond-shaped panes of the Dutch window wasn't very good, but Polly was accustomed to reading in worse light.

The book she was reading was a cheaply made and poorly printed pamphlet entitled: *America's Reply to English Injustices*. The name of the author wasn't given. In August 1774, that would have been far too dangerous. Men had already been imprisoned for less. Like most of the political tracts flooding the colonies at the moment, it was very popular. Ethan said that nearly fifty thousand copies of it had been sold.

Polly had already read nearly all of it, and she understood why people liked it. It was very easy to read. Even a child could understand it. And the things it said were simple and clear and almost always made sense.

Why should we pay taxes if we have no voice in the government that imposes the taxes? It was as simple as that. England was far away, burdened with age and inflexible custom. Here was a new world. Here was the beginning of everything. People had a chance here in America to start out in new directions. For the first time in human history there was a chance for every man to stand up tall in liberty . . .

Polly lifted her gaze from the printed page and stared at the window. She had a very good mind, but it was a feminine mind, and, as such, inclined to be concerned with things more immediately important than human liberty. She was pleased that Ethan had brought her a gift from the largest city in the Colonies. It was the first time he had ever given her anything. But he had also brought Kathy two gifts, entrusting them to Polly to give her sister, since he was not allowed to see Kathy at all.

When Kathy had undone the bundles she had squealed with delight. Ethan had brought her three fashion dolls from Paris. They were all very beautiful and dressed in the latest modes. From them Kathy would be able to copy a whole flock of smart new dresses. Fashion dolls were the only way a fine lady had of knowing what was being worn in the great European capitals.

His second gift to Kathy was even more extravagant: he had managed to purchase a packet of five hundred pins. Polly knew how much straight pins for sewing cost. Since each pin was made by hand one at a time, they were expensive luxuries, especially in the American colonies, because most of them had to be brought from abroad. Polly guessed that this packet of pins must have cost Ethan more than ten pounds.

But it wasn't so much the comparative cost of the gifts. True enough, the pamphlet had cost Ethan only a few shillings. What troubled Polly was the question of whether or not she should be flattered because Ethan considered her a person with a mind, rather than a silly girl to be beguiled with dolls and pins.

After half a moment's reflection, she decided not to be flattered. There wasn't a man alive who gave two hoots up a hollow stump what went on inside a girl's head. As long as the exterior was perfumed and soft and pleasant, men were more than satisfied. Polly knew well that most men were frightened by a brainy girl. That they regarded her as a kind of freak.

Polly swore under her breath and hurled the unfinished book—little more than a pamphlet really—halfway across the room. She wasn't supposed to know how to swear, but she did. In the 1770s, the most genteel lady alive couldn't escape such knowledge, because she had only to go to her window to hear at any hour of the day the very air being blistered blue with thunderous oaths. In the hard-drinking, hard-riding Colonies, profanity was a fine art.

"Polly," her father said sternly, "why are you throwing your books around?"

Polly hadn't heard him come up the stairs. She had been too intent with her reading. Wordlessly she watched him stoop and pick up the pamphlet. He took his square, steel-rimmed spectacles out of his pocket and fitted them over his eyes.

"*America's Reply to English Injustices!*" he roared. "Who gave you this trash?"

"I—I found it," Polly lied. "It was lying on the ground right in front of the house, Papa . . ."

"Where some mischief-maker had dropped it on purpose," Patrick said, "with the intent that some member of my household should find it. I've often remarked your bad temper, missy, and reproved you upon it. But this time you're right, lass. You did well to throw away this miserable pack of lies . . ."

"Are they lies, Papa?" Polly said. "I—I don't like what that man says, but they sound awfully like the truth to me. . . ."

Patrick Knowles sat heavily down upon the end of the bed.

"They are the subtlest kind of lies, Polly," he said gently, "because they contain a grain of truth in them. Our Government has made its mistakes. But they remain just that—errors, not villainy. 'Tis upon the other side that the villainy lies . . ."

"How so, Papa?"

"All this trouble was started in Boston, where, as you know, I also have offices. A man named John Hancock lives there. He has a great name, comes from one of the finest families. But that didn't prevent him from being a common smuggler. The whole trouble started when he tried to prevent the customs officials from collecting duty on wine he'd brought from Madeira . . ."

He went on slowly, telling her the story. How the riot had grown out of the seizure of Hancock's sloop *Liberty*. How the customs officials had been forced to flee Boston. How, as a result of this plain and defiant disobedience of the laws of their sovereign, the occupation had been brought upon the town.

Polly listened to him wonderingly. She had never felt

so close to her father before. For the first time in her young life, he was taking the trouble to talk to her like an equal, a grownup. She felt a great wave of tenderness for this big, baffled man.

"I'll admit the rebels have much justice in their claim that the laws are unwise, even unfair," he went on, "but until those laws are repealed, a good subject has no other recourse but to obey them. I have written my representatives in London to petition Parliament for their repeal. But until those pleas are heard, I shall do my duty by the Crown . . ."

"But, Papa, if we had our own representatives in Parliament . . ."

"We will one day," Patrick Knowles said. "If we have patience. But 'tis not that these firebrands want. They want independence! Freedom, they call it. Freedom to be swallowed up by France or Spain. Where would we be now, had we not His Majesty's Navies to defend us?"

"But, Papa," Polly put in, "the soldiers in Boston were cruel. They—they abused women—and they shot people . . ."

"After they were grossly provoked. That miserable little failure Sam Adams—I knew him well—used a motley gathering of riotous blackguards to create martyrs for his piddling cause! Know you, missy, who these martyrs were? Drunken sailors from the waterfront, idlers, vagrants, bond servants—even Negroes! They stoned the soldiers of our King. 'Twas no wonder they were fired upon . . . And that business of the tea that they threw into the harbor: the East Indian Company had huge surpluses of tea. They were actually offering it to us at lower prices than Hancock and the other smugglers could afford to take for their smuggled brew! Hancock has never admitted that he had mountains of smuggled tea from Holland in his warehouses—that he stood to lose a fortune if he was undersold! Hence his fine, patriotic fervor—proclaiming it all a trick to destroy competition, arousing the people to piracy and destruction. I tell you, missy, these rebels have many sins upon their heads!"

After he was gone, Polly was puzzled. Patrick Knowles hadn't lied. She knew that. But then, neither had Ethan. And Ethan was drunk with the idea of liberty. He was afire with freedom's holy flame.

She had to know. At fifteen, Polly was still too young to realize that the whole of right never lies on any one side of a quarrel, that men with legitimate disputes always tend to blackguard their opponents, making of a difference of opinion the blackest villainy. Especially when that difference hurt their purses. Ah yes, especially then. . . .

So she did the only thing possible under the circumstances. She sought out Ethan. That was very easy for her because of the habit her whole family had of regarding her as a child. They didn't watch her coming and going the same way they watched Kathy's.

An hour later, she was riding with Ethan through the wooded section north of the city. He talked to her gaily about Philadelphia, the biggest city in America.

"They paint their shop fronts in the brightest colors," he laughed, "red, blue, green, or yellow. And the signs on the taverns, you've never seen such colors, Pol. Their clothes, too. Don't believe that story about Quakers wearing sober garb. They dress as fine as anyone else. Finer, maybe. Why some of the people actually hooted at me and at the delegate from New Jersey because we wore no wigs!"

"What did you do while you were there, Ethan?" Polly asked.

"Went to the Fish House Club and had Fish House Punch. The next morning I had to retrieve my head. It was over in the corner being kicked around by the cat."

"Now really, Ethan!"

"A fact. He put some new lumps on it—see?"

"You're awful. Are the girls—pretty?"

"Beautiful. I fell in love sixteen times."

"Prettier," Polly whispered, "than Kathy?"

Ethan looked at her. His blue eyes were grave.

"Nobody could be prettier than Kathy," he said quietly. "Nobody—in all the world. . . ."

Polly looked at him a long, slow time. What she was feeling couldn't be said. Not in words—not in any such words as she knew how to say. Ethan saw her face, and started talking again, quickly.

"I wasn't allowed to attend the Congress," he said. "Father took care of that. So I went dancing. Met a man from Virginia—named Washington. I've never seen a man who loved to dance more than he. Good at it, too. The girls loved to dance with him, in spite of the fact that he was a big, homely cuss with a face all scarred up from smallpox. He danced with a mechanic's daughter for an hour one night. Scandalized everybody. Think it scandalized him a little, but he loved it. Actually he's the most aristocratic man I ever met. He's a delegate. Father swore that he was almost a King's man because he tried so hard to prevent the others from doing anything serious about England. Truth to tell, that Colonel Washington is more afraid of the common people getting out of hand than he is of the lobster-backs . . ."

"Why do you talk so much about him?"

Ethan looked at her, and his eyes were puzzled.

"I guess it's because he impressed me more than anyone else I met. More even than Patrick Henry, who can make music out of words. But Henry said one great thing, though: 'I am not a Virginian,' he told them, 'but an American!' That's what I am," Ethan added quietly, "an American. One of the first Americans . . ."

"You're proud of that, aren't you?" Polly said. "But Papa is just as proud of being a subject of the King."

"I know," Ethan said. "Your father is a fine man, Polly. A little too rigid, but a man of honor. Too bad he's on the wrong side . . ."

"Is he, Eth? He said that your patriots were a band of thieves and smugglers. He said they were less concerned about—America than with feathering their own nests. He even said that those people who were killed in that massacre in Boston were nothing but scum—redemptioners, drunkards, Negro slaves . . ."

Ethan's eyes made blue lightning under the dark trees.

He rose in the stirrups and pointed with his crop.

"See that man?" he said.

Polly looked where he was pointing. A black man was cutting firewood. He was a big man with muscles that coiled and uncoiled like ebony cables as he worked. His ax rose in a smooth arc, came whistling down, bit. The wood flew apart. He was singing. His voice rolled under the trees deep and slow and sad.

"Scum?" Ethan said, and his own voice was tight in

his throat so that the words came jetting out like musket balls. "People, Pol. Never forget that. Redemptioners who had to sell themselves for a number of years to buy their passage across toward ultimate freedom. Drunkards—yes. Show me a man who doesn't like a glass upon occasion and you've shown me no man at all. Slaves like that man. But whom does slavery disgrace—its victims, or the men who've so armored their hearts with self-interest that they can buy and sell other men like cattle and feel no shame?"

Looking at him, Polly wasn't confused any more. What her father had said was logic, and what Ethan was saying was feeling. The choice was no choice at all. Feeling was always better than logic. Finer, nobler, right. She hadn't thought it was possible for her to love Ethan any more than she did already. But great waves started out from somewhere near the region of her heart and spread to the very tips of her fingers and her toes. She couldn't breathe. She hurt. She wanted to cry, but she couldn't let Ethan see her crying. Yet the noise in her ears was like singing.

"Slaves," Ethan went on more quietly. "I wonder if we'll ever build a monument to one of them—to a man who was a slave or the son of a slave, I don't know which . . ."

"Why, Eth?"

"Because the first man to die on Boston Commons was a mulatto. The first blood to water the tree of liberty was pumped from the shot-torn heart of a man to whom we had denied anything like liberty. I think God let it happen like that to remind us to search our hearts and be humble and to love. . . ."

He was intensely moved. Polly could see that. Suddenly he spurred his horse forward and dismounted next to the woodcutter. The big man was putting the wood into a little handcart. Without a word, Ethan stooped and began to help him fill his cart.

The Negro stared at him.

"Baas," he got out, pronouncing the word Dutch fashion, "I don't need no help. 'Sides, you'll ruin your clothes."

Ethan smiled.

"Hang my clothes," he said. "And you do need help. All men do—all men who are brothers. . . ."

The big Negro came closer, peering anxiously into Ethan's face.

"Baas," he said, "you sure you feel all right?"

Ethan laughed. The sound of his laughter to Polly was like sunlight, lancing among the trees.

"I feel fine," Ethan said. "Never felt better in all my life. Besides I'm not doing this for you—exactly. I'm doing it for a man to whom I owe a debt. A man named Attucks from Boston. Crispus Attucks. Remember that name, will you?"

"Yes, baas," the big Negro said, "I'll remember that name."

Polly got down from her horse. She walked up to Ethan and began to brush the dirt and bits of bark off his clothes. When she spoke her voice was tight, strangled.

"Ethan," she said, "I'm going to kiss you. I'm sorry, but I've got to . . ."

When they rode on through the woods, Polly was crying very quietly. Ethan's face was still and sad.

"Don't cry, Polly," he said.

"Can't help it. This is twice I've been a shameless

baggage and hurled myself at your head. I wish I didn't love you. But I do. I can't help that either—any more than you can help being you—so tall and wonderful and kind . . ."

"I—I'm very fond of you, Polly," Ethan said lamely. "Maybe one day I'll get over Kathy . . ."

"You're a fool!" Polly said bitterly. "What good is it to love a girl who broke her engagement to you because she was told to? What good, Ethan?"

Ethan smiled at her a little sadly.

"What good is it to love a man whose heart is occupied elsewhere, little Polly? Love's a funny thing. You can't just blow it out like a candle and relight it again. It goes on burning whether you want it to, or not. Besides, I'm going to tell you something, Polly, because I trust you. I've seen Kathy several times since that incident. She swears she loves me still; she believes your father will relent . . ."

"He'll never relent, Ethan," Polly said. "You just don't know him. I don't think you know Kathy either —but no matter. I—I hope you two will be—very—happy . . ."

Then she put down her head and really cried.

Ethan let her cry. There was nothing else he could do.

Polly didn't see Ethan again until Sunday of that same week. She was sitting alone in the family pew at Trinity Church. But she wasn't paying any attention to the sermon. She could think of two dozen places she would rather have been than in church on this hot September morning, but she was resigned to being there. That was one of the things that came of being a Knowles.

Ordinarily her whole family would have been there with her. But her father was abed with one of his attacks of gout and her mother had stayed at home to wait on him. Kathy, being Kathy, had taken advantage of the situation. She'd left the house to go to church with Polly, but on the way they had met Susie Lawrence, and Kathy had skipped off with her, after getting Polly to swear she wouldn't tell.

Polly glanced toward the Pages' pew. It had been empty when she came in, but now Daniel Page was in it. Polly sighed a little. She had hoped that Ethan would be there, too.

The sermon roared and thundered on. Polly heard scarcely a word of it. She wondered what ministers would do if they ever ran out of hell-fire and damnation. Not much chance of that, though. The supply seemed inexhaustible.

She looked openly at Mr. Page. Ethan was very like his father, except that Daniel was in some ways handsomer than his son. His silvery hair became him, contrasting pleasantly with the coppery skin that Ethan had gotten from him. He was broader than Ethan, and a little shorter. Even sitting there without moving he gave the impression of strength.

Ethan's more graceful, Polly thought. But he'll age well, too; getting better-looking as he grows older, just like Mr. Page. And he'll have the same kind of face with the wrinkles in it that come from smiling, not frowning. That's the trouble with Papa. The older he gets, the meaner he looks . . . and that's a shame because he isn't really mean at all.

When the services were over at last, and the number of the saved had been so reduced that Polly wondered why God took the trouble, she saw Mr. Page coming toward her.

"An unexpected pleasure, Miss Polly," he said. "May I have the honor of escorting you home? 'Tisn't often an old gaffer like me has the chance to talk to a pretty girl without having her beaux, or even his own son, interfere."

Polly smiled. Daniel Page was one of the nicest men she knew.

"I haven't any beaux, Mr. Page," she said. "And, as for Ethan—I'm afraid he isn't interested."

"But you are, aren't you, Polly?" Dan Page said kindly. "I've known that a long time. Ethan's a fool. Any man who works in metals should be able to tell tinsel from sterling worth. Your sister's pretty, but you're something better than that. You're fine. The metal's solid, and unalloyed—all the way through. And it's pure gold . . ."

"Thank you," Polly said.

"Come," Daniel Page said, and took her arm.

"Mr. Page," Polly murmured, "you'd—I'd better not. My father . . ."

"Right," Dan Page laughed. "I'd forgotten how seriously Pat takes his politics. But come by the shop with me. I have something for you."

Polly thought about that. If anyone saw her walking with Mr. Page and told her father, she'd be in trouble. But there was the chance that she might see Ethan. And what could her father do but scold her, anyhow?

"All right," she said, and Dan Page took her arm.

The Pages' Pewter Foundry and Silver Smithy was on Pine Street near Nassau. It was small, but at that it was the biggest such works in all of New York. Most foundries were small enough to be run by the owner and one or two sons, but the Pages employed no less than ten workers.

Daniel Page unlocked the door to the shop. The foundry was directly behind the shop in the same building, but since it was Sunday, the furnaces were banked and the smoke and smells that Polly had always found exciting were absent.

A man stood up as they entered the shop. Polly knew why Daniel Page kept a watchman there, even on Sundays. His pewter and silver ware were valuable, and keeping the Sabbath meant little to thieves.

"Here it is, Miss Polly," Dan Page said, and took up a syrup pitcher made of heavy silver.

Polly took the pitcher, but she didn't look at it. She was staring at the watchman. She didn't like the way he looked at her. There was something in his face like— like rage, Polly realized suddenly.

Then she recognized the man. He was Jason Goodby, a former employee of her father's. And Patrick Knowles had had him put in prison for not paying his debts.

The amount of money involved had been quite small, Polly remembered. She had begged her father to forgive poor Jason. But Patrick Knowles wasn't a man to forgive easily. His justice was never tempered with mercy.

Dan Page followed her gaze.

"Jason," he said quietly, "that business of your imprisonment is closed, d'you hear me? And you'd best let it remain so."

"Harkee, Mr. Page," Jason said. "Ye're a good man —that ye be and no mistake. But when I see this maid o' his in her silks and laces, it minds me of how my poor Fanny died—of hunger, missy! Whilst I was in prison, unable to earn her bread——"

"Jason!" Daniel Page interrupted.

"No, Mr. Page," Polly said, "don't silence him." She walked toward Jason. When she was close she could see that he was trembling.

"Mr. Goodby," she said, "I am sorry for my father's harshness toward you. I tried to dissuade him, but I could not. Yet it seems to me that you are being unjust when you blame me for something that I could nowise help . . ."

"Polly!" Ethan's voice came through the doorway. "Thank God! I had almost given up hope . . ."

"What ails you, lad?" Dan Page said.

"There's been violence, Father," Ethan told him. "Scattered as yet—but all over the city. You remember you marked with disfavor some of the wilder elements who've attached themselves to our cause. Well now they've shown their hand. They've attacked the homes of King's men. And only this morning they displayed their valor by molesting two or three Tory maids in the streets . . ."

"Good!" Jason Goodby said.

"Nay, lad," Daniel Page said sternly. "Our cause is just, but such things debase it. Ethan, you'd better see Miss Polly home . . ."

"I meant to," Ethan said. "I'll meet you at home, Father. I think we'd better take counsel with some of the others . . ."

"Right," Daniel Page said.

They had turned into William Street before Polly remembered her pitcher. It was too late now. It was far too late for most ordinary things.

"Tell your father," Ethan said, "not to drive abroad in the big coach. They've signaled out coaches and other such marks of wealth. Above all, he shouldn't take either you or Kathy with him . . ."

"I'll tell him," Polly said.

But Patrick Knowles only snorted. To show his defiance, he took them for a drive the very next afternoon.

They hadn't gone three blocks before the first stone crashed through the window of the carriage, showering them with broken glass.

At once the coachman drew up the four. That was a mistake; for the next instant, they were surrounded.

Polly recognized the leader of the mob. He was Jason Goodby.

"King's man!" Jason roared. "Damned Tory! Take that!"

Another stone came through the window and struck Patrick in the face, bringing blood.

"Ain't he pretty!" another of the dirty workmen laughed. "Nice plum-colored coat. Harkee, boys! That there coat's out o' fashion. What say we give 'im a new one—black, say—tar black, with some pretty feathers in it?"

A dozen hands tore at the door. Then they were reeling away from the coach, using both hands to shield their heads, for Ethan Page stood tall in the stirrups and belabored them right and left with his crop.

"Eth!" Jason got out. "Thought you was with us!"

"I am," Ethan said sternly, "until you make war on old men and women. Save your strength, boys, for the lobsterbacks. That will prove you are men. To behave like a pack of yapping dogs shames our cause in the eyes of all men of good will . . ."

They slunk away from the coach. Ethan rode beside the carriage until they came back to the house. Then he dismounted and helped Kathy and Polly down.

But Patrick Knowles refused his hand.

"I thank you for your aid, young sir," he said, "but until your opinions change, there can be no fellowship between us."

Ethan stared at him.

"My opinions are my own, sir," he said softly, "but yours, I think, have greater need of mending, since they have endangered not only your life, but Kathy's . . ."

"Damned impudent puppy!" Patrick snarled. "Yours will but earn you a tall gibbet, whereon you'll kick beside your sire!"

"Papa!" Polly gasped.

"Good day, sir, and ladies," Ethan murmured. "I trust you'll remember, Mr. Knowles, that patriots can build as lofty gallows as King's men. But no matter. If you had had any respect for common men, you'd not have thrown poor Jason into debtors' prison and earned his hate—such errors can be fatal. . . ."

He bowed deeply, and fixed his three-cornered hat atop his black head with a most jaunty air. Then he mounted and cantered off down William Street.

Watching him go, Polly had to blink her eyes very hard. One thing Ethan had said stuck in her mind like a burr: ". . . endangered not only your life, but Kathy's . . ." Not your life and both your daughters'. Not Kathy's and Polly's lives. Just Kathy's.

He doesn't, she wailed inside her heart, care if I live or die! I hate him! I hate . . .

But even as she thought that, she knew it wasn't so.

She had to put a scarf around her shoulders now, when she went into the garden. The air had a bite in it. It was going to be winter soon; but Polly, who loved the clean snows, didn't look forward to it with any joy. She had always loved the sleigh rides, flying behind the swift horses, and skating on the ponds in the wooded section north of the city. But she was almost sixteen now, and such things seemed to her very childish. She didn't stop to remember that New Yorkers of all ages engaged in these winter sports.

She sat very still on the bench near the dovecot and reflected with painful honesty that a broken heart wasn't a disease you died of. That was the bad part about it. It just went on and on, a slow dull ache that covered her whole body, except that her heart seemed to hurt a little more than the rest of her. She sat there a long time, giving vent to the luxury of self-pity. In December, she'd be sixteen, old enough to become engaged. But what good was that going to do when the only man on earth for her was in love with Kathy? What possible good?

It was really cold now. Polly made a move to get up and go back into the house. But then she heard the voices. One of them was Kathy's. Kathy was crying.

"Oh, Ethan," she sobbed, "no!"

"I have to, my love," Ethan said gently. "Our group has decided to send me on to Boston to get in touch with Adams and Hancock and others of our leaders there . . ."

"Those filthy old Sons of Liberty," Kathy stormed. "I wish they were all dead!"

"If they were, then I'd be dead, too, Kathy," Ethan said, "for I am one of them."

"I wish I didn't love you," Kathy pouted. "I should have more sense than to be in love with a traitor. It's awful, Ethan! It really is. I have nightmares. I'm always dreaming that I'm standing somewhere near a gallows and a group of the King's soldiers are leading you up to it to be h-hh-hanged! Ethan, dearest, give up this madness. All the best people, all the decent, respectable people are for the King. How can you stand the rabble you associate with now? Beggars, cobblers, clerks, servants, vagrants, slaves! How can you bear the smell of them?"

"Better," Ethan said grimly, "than I can the perfume of unearned wealth, for that's a kind of harlotry . . ."

"Ethan!"

"Sorry. But we're trying to make a kind of world where there won't be any beggars or slaves, Kathy. Where honest workmen can't be thrown into prison for debt. Where men obey only laws of their own making, not every whim of a king! We'll be taxed then, to be sure; but justly, because our own representatives will be there to see that the taxes don't exceed the bounds of reason or of sense. And our goods will be carried in our own ships, without let or hindrance. I tell you, Kathy ——"

"And I tell you something, Mr. Ethan Page! You're mad, and my father was right to make me give you back your ring!"

Ethan didn't say anything for a long time. When he spoke his voice was so low that Polly had to strain her ears to hear it.

"You think so, Kathy?" he said. "Then you leave me no other course but to agree with you."

He turned and started to walk away from Kathy.

Polly held her breath. She didn't dare move. She hoped he wouldn't see her sitting there, or else he'd realize that she'd overheard the whole conversation. And that was a base thing.

He came on, walking straight toward her.

"Ethan!" Kathy called.

He stopped.

"Ethan Page, you come back here!"

Slowly Ethan turned and went back to where Kathy stood.

Polly let her breath out slowly. She stood up, took a step on tiptoe. Then she halted. She had to look back. She knew she shouldn't, but she couldn't help it.

"Darling," Kathy was crying, "I don't care whether you are mad or not. I don't even care if you're a traitor. I love you. That's all that counts, isn't it? Let's not quarrel anymore over things that don't concern us . . . Just love me, Ethan—that's all I ask . . ."

She put out her arms to him, and he came to her.

Polly got up and ran out of the garden. She clawed open the back door of the house, and half fell over a chair in the hallway. She couldn't see. It wasn't until an hour later that it came to her that she had gotten some good out of the experience.

She would at least know where Ethan was going.

But it was not Polly who arranged things to the ultimate satisfaction of all parties concerned. It was Kathy—with the aid of that motley, unwashed horde of tattered rapscallions who called themselves the Sons of Liberty.

Not that they intended to aid Kathy's schemes. The only thing they ever wanted to do with a Tory miss was to besmatter her face with whiskery kisses, clip off her hair, and subject her to other familiarities if the opportunity presented itself.

"Papa," Kathy said at breakfast, "why don't we all go up to Uncle Peter's in Boston? We'd be much safer there. After all, we'd have the King's soldiers for protection . . ."

Patrick Knowles glared at her over the top of his square spectacles.

"I have never run from a fight in my life," he boomed. "If these thieving scoundrels want trouble, they will find it here!"

That should have ended the matter, but it didn't. On Wednesday, the Knowles had been invited to sup with the Lawrences. Old Major Lawrence was as stout a King's man as Patrick Knowles himself.

On Wednesday evening, Patrick sat in his study and smoked his long pipe and gazed frequently at his watch and swore at the mysterious inability of women ever to get dressed on time. He should have been used to it by now, but he wasn't. Afterwards, he should have been grateful for his wife's and his daughters' tardiness, because it probably saved his life.

The Lawrences lived on Green Street. When the Knowleses rounded the corner, the first thing they heard was the smashing of glass and women screaming.

Patrick turned beet red and started to jump from the carriage. But Polly and Kathy seized his arms.

"No, Papa!" Polly said. "Why, you have only a penknife!"

"Get the carriage out of here!" Kathy screamed. "If they see it, they'll attack us, too!"

The coachman whirled the heavy coach about and started out of Green Street at a gallop. But before they had gone very far, Patrick ordered him to stop.

"Take the girls home," he ordered. "I must see after my friends."

Polly was proud of her father. Whatever faults Patrick Knowles may have had, he was nobody's coward. But the minute he stepped out of the coach, she jumped down beside him.

"Polly!" he thundered. "Get back in that——"

He never finished his words. The big coach rumbled away, leaving the two of them standing there.

"Damme, missy!" he exploded. "Now what on earth ——"

"Don't worry, Papa," Polly grinned, "I have to take care of you."

In spite of himself, Patrick had to smile at her. There was a warm spot in his heart for this spunky younger daughter of his.

"Should have been a boy," he grumbled. "Come along, then."

They kept close to the walls until they had almost reached the house. The Sons of Liberty were parading in and out of the smashed doors of the Lawrences' house, laden with silver and linens and household furnishings and fine clothes. Some of them had dressed themselves in feminine finery. One drunken little fellow had on a pair of lacy woman's underwear, the ruffles of the long pantaloons sticking out grotesquely about his ankles. Others were running back and forth from the stables hurling shovelfuls of refuse and animal dung through the smashed windows.

They had led the Major's fine horse around in front of the house. Six of them were busily engaged in painting the animal. They were making his body bright red, his head light blue, and his tail a glorious yellow.

Polly had to laugh.

"Don't look!" her father roared.

But Polly looked.

They had stripped fat old Major Lawrence stark-naked. They led him out of the house and forced him to mount his gorgeous horse. Then they led Mrs. Lawrence and Susie Lawrence out behind him. They had been kinder to the women. They had allowed them to keep on their stays and petticoats. But they had clipped off all their hair. Then they tied them to the horse's tail, and the dark little man in the woman's pantaloons caught hold of the bridle.

"Forward march!" he called. Then the whole procession started off down the street, followed by the Major's own carts piled high with stolen goods, followed by the drunken rabble with the Major's guns and fowling pieces clapped to their shoulders, with still other grinning roisterers bringing up the rear by driving away all the Major's livestock.

"How awful!" Polly breathed. "Papa, what are we going to do?"

Patrick Knowles' brick-colored face was even redder than usual.

"I'll show you, missy!" he snorted, and Polly could see him getting set for a rush.

Then she remembered the rebels' guns. Her father, always a law-abiding citizen, despite his temper, had nothing more than a small penknife in his pocket. He was no coward, Polly knew, but a brave man armed only with a penknife would not be much help to the Lawrences now.

Patrick dug his heels into the ground. But Polly was quicker. She threw herself down across his path so that he fell over the minute he started after the rabble. Both their clothes were ruined.

"Thunderation!" Patrick roared.

"Oh, Papa," Polly said, "you're the bravest man alive, and I love you; but I can't let you get yourself killed! They've got guns and we haven't. . . ."

The rebels had turned at the noise of their fall, and all the guns were already pointed at them. Looking into those gun muzzles made Patrick Knowles see the sense in his daughter's words. Then the rebels grinned and lowered their firearms.

"Just an old drunk fighting with his daughter," one of them laughed. "Git along now, boys!"

"Dangblast them to eternal tarnation!" Patrick spluttered. "I'll——"

"You'll come home with me now," Polly said, "and get some brandy and greatcoats. The Lawrences are going to need them. . . ."

They found Major Lawrence tied to a tree in the woods north of the city; it took them until nightfall to find him. His wife and daughter were bound to another tree near by.

Polly was right; they needed the brandy and the greatcoats. The Major was blue with cold. By the time Polly and her father got them home, the old man was already running a temperature. Four days later he died, as much, Polly suspected, from mortification and helpless rage as from the pneumonia that finally strangled him.

Polly wept at his funeral. In her heart of hearts she knew that Ethan would never have condoned what the rebels had done to the Lawrence family. He, she told herself, would have chased those thieving blackguards singlehanded out of that street. But, she wailed, how could he ever have joined forces with such men?

Then it came to her that Ethan hadn't joined forces with them, that when the chips were down, men like these would run like rats at the first sound of gunfire, and only the true patriots would be left, the real lovers of liberty. And liberty, being herself a thing of total purity, could never be besmirched by the scoundrels who mouthed her name in vain.

The whole thing had one happy result. The day after the funeral, Kathy and Polly and Susie and their mothers found themselves on the stage, bound for Boston.

Patrick Knowles watched them go. Then he went back into his barricaded house and oiled and loaded his guns.

CHAPTER 3

Polly Knowles looked over to where Susie Lawrence sat gazing up at young Peyton Cranbrooke with adoring eyes.

Sue's happy now, she thought, while—while I just sit here by the window and wait for Ethan to pass by so I can see him. And it's no comfort that I'm absolutely sure that he will pass sooner or later. What good does it do me to sit here and wait for him, when he only passes in the hope of catching a glimpse of Kathy? I'm a fool. Susie's right. Peyton is a nice boy. Lieutenant Peyton Cranbrooke, of His Majesty's Royal Marines. Well, why not? It's not his fault. He's only following orders—just as Ethan's obeying the commands of his side. . . .

I wonder when the fighting's going to start? It's sure to, Ethan says. I only hope that nothing happens to Ethan. It's been so long . . . Let's see . . . We came to Uncle Peter's in November, and it's April now. April 1775. . . .

She heard Kathy laugh, and turned toward her. Didn't take Kathy long, did it? she thought bitterly. Of course, Cecil's handsome; but so is Ethan. Is it his good looks that intrigue Kathy—or his title? Major Cecil Fitzgerald, Viscount Linkletter. Very fine. The Lady Katherine, Viscountess Linkletter. She'd like that, Kathy would.

47

Polly shook her head, as if to clear it. I'm mean, she told herself sternly, mean and unfair. Any girl would like it. And almost anyone would like Cecil. Kathy can't help being Kathy any more than I can help being myself. Kathy is vain, and thoughtless, and fickle—but she's never intentionally unkind—while I often am. She loves me, I think, as much as she's capable of loving anyone. While I—Lord forgive me—have come very close to hating her lately. What an ugly thing jealousy is!

She saw Cecil get up with that languid grace of his and saunter over to where her uncle Peter sat beside her mother.

He was very fine in his scarlet uniform. He was tall and slender, and almost too graceful for a man. And he was handsome—wonderfully handsome. He'd left off his wig, and his close-cropped blond hair curled in ringlets above his high forehead. He reminded Polly of a painting she had seen once of Apollo. Only Cecil was better-looking, if anything.

"I say, old chap," he said to Peter Knowles, "this love business is deuced catching, what? Just thought I'd better remind you that the lady is still married—and to your brother, I'm told."

Peter Knowles turned brick red. Polly's uncle was good-looking too. In fact, there was not a man present at Susie's engagement party that sixth day of April 1775, who was not far above the average in appearance.

"Damme, lad!" Peter laughed. "You're a mind reader! First time I've ever regretted my single state. And if Pat weren't my brother——"

"Ach, Piet!" Gertrude smiled. "How you do talk! An

old *goede vrouw* like me—almost a grandmother, yet
..."

"Not so fast, Mistress Knowles!" Cecil said. "Let us
not be hasty. You're overlooking one minor detail,
aren't you? Neither your charming Polly, nor the sur-
passingly lovely Katherine is as yet married—or even
spoken for ..."

"And whose fault is that?" Gertrude laughed. "Will-
ing I am to rock their *kinder* to sleep, but a man they
must catch for themselves. So look oudt, Cecil!"

"Mama!" Kathy said.

Cecil strolled over to her and sat down upon the arm
of her chair.

"I rather think I shouldn't run very fast, Kathy," he
said tenderly, "were I eligible for such bliss ..."

"And aren't you?" Kathy asked boldly.

"I am wedded to danger, my sweet," Cecil quipped.
"To danger and to death ..."

He looked at Polly.

"And you, dear Polly?" he said, mockingly. "Haven't
you yet made your choice? Which man among us will
you honor with your favor?"

"None of you," Polly said tartly. "I'm an American,
and you're the enemies of my country."

"Polly Knowles!" her uncle Peter thundered.

"Don't scold her, Mr. Knowles," Cecil smiled. "D'you
know what we call her? Mistress Rebel. And we always
whistle 'Yankee Doodle' at her. But I know your secret,
sweet Polly. 'Tis that lanky, blue-jawed Yankee lad,
isn't it? The one who's forever mooning after Kathy,
here. Can't say I admire your taste, Miss Polly. But I
think we can arrange matters, can't we, Katherine?
You'll give her the fellow, won't you?"

"Gladly," Kathy laughed.

Polly got up and walked out of the room. She remembered how sad Ethan's face was now. That hurt Polly. She wanted him to be happy, not sad. She even had some vague, enchanting ideas about how she would make him so. She thought about how nice it would be to brew Ethan's tea for him and bring him coals from the fireplace to light his pipe. She'd make him rum fustians on cold winter evenings, too, and—— But beyond that her mind could not go.

She stood by the window in the hall and waited until he rode by as he always did, every day, hoping to see Kathy. He could ride anywhere, even in Boston, because the patriots far outnumbered the Tories, and it had been demonstrated that the presence of the British Army was scant protection against a horsewhipping, smashed coach windows, or having one's house burned down about one's ears. The Tories didn't interfere with the patriots, and the British Army could only act after some overt deed such as the rioting on the common that had come to be called the Boston Massacre. . . .

But he couldn't enter the house. Patrick Knowles had informed his brother by mail of the broken engagement, and asked him to forbid Ethan the house, if he should follow Kathy to Boston. Peter Knowles heartily agreed with his brother on all political questions, and could be counted on to obey this request. Polly was less sure of her mother, though. Gertrude Knowles had always liked her prospective son-in-law. But she was Dutch, born and bred, and whatever her private opinions were, to disobey the expressed command of her husband was as unthinkable to her as murder.

Today, however, Ethan wasn't alone. He had a small dark man with him. Polly ran out of the house.

"Ethan!" she called to him.

Ethan turned in the saddle and a slow grin lighted his eyes. He got down from the horse and the other man got down after him. Polly liked the little man at once. He had such a keen, exciting face.

"Paul," Ethan said, "I want you to meet the best female patriot in the country, Miss Polly Knowles. Polly, may I present Paul Revere?"

"Knowles?" Paul Revere said, and frowned. "But all the Knowles hereabouts are——"

"King's men, Tories," Polly sighed. "My uncle, my father. All except me."

Revere smiled.

"Now I know we'll whip the lobsterbacks. At the sight of so pretty a patriot, they'll all lay down their arms."

Polly dropped him a curtsy. Then she looked at Ethan.

"Take me riding with you, Ethan," she said.

"But Polly, it's late and your uncle——"

"Won't miss me for hours. They're having a party. Even Mama and Mistress Lawrence have put away so much Madeira that they won't even think of looking in my room until morning . . ."

"What about a horse?"

"Ride around back and tell Tim I said to saddle the mare for me. I'll wait here . . ."

She turned and smiled at Paul Revere.

"You're an artist, aren't you Mr. Revere?"

Revere looked puzzled.

"That's one sin I've never before been accused of," he said. "Why did you think I was?"

"I saw a picture you drew. Ethan showed it to me. It was called 'The Horrid Massacre in Boston.' You are the same Revere, aren't you?"

"Guilty as charged. But Sam Adams asked me to do that because I'm an engraver, not an artist. If you looked at it closely, you'd see it's very badly drawn . . ."

Ethan came around the house leading Polly's mare. Both of them helped Polly to mount.

"You know, Polly," Ethan said as they moved off, "if it hadn't been for Paul here, I doubt I'd ever have gotten into Boston . . ."

"Why?" Polly asked.

"I knew of him through the organization. Therefore I took some fine drawings of silver and pewter ware, bronze doorknobs, knockers, and the like along with me. When the British sentries stopped me, I got them to take me to their officer. He was a man of sense and taste. I told him I was going to consult with my colleague Revere on the best method of casting them. And I had to actually do it, because that British Major wrote an order on six of my finest designs for Paul to make for him. They've already been shipped back to his wife in London!"

Revere smiled.

"I neglected to mention that along with my engraving, I also do a little silversmithing . . ."

"A little!" Ethan snorted. "Paul's the finest silversmith in the Colonies. Paul, let's ride by your shop so I can show Polly some of your pieces . . ."

"With pleasure," Paul Revere said.

They sat in the little shop and Polly looked at the pitchers, platters, bowls, salt shakers, knobs, hinges, and knockers. They were all very simple and plain. But as young as she was, and accustomed to ornamentation, Polly saw they were very fine. For the first time she realized how pure mass and form and line could be exquisite. Paul Revere's feeling for harmony and balance was lyrical.

"You know," she said to him, "you didn't tell the truth, Mr. Revere. You are an artist. A very great artist."

Paul winked at Ethan.

"I also ride horses," he said.

"That he does," Ethan laughed. "He's the messenger who brought the Suffolk Resolutions to the Continental Congress. They flatly proclaimed independence for Massachusetts. I think that's what Paul's going to be known as—the Messenger of the Revolution . . ."

"You're not such a bad rider yourself," Paul Revere said.

"Thanks," Ethan replied. "You know, Polly, there are six or seven of us who're standing by. The minute anything happens, we're to ride through the countryside and spread the alarm. Then the Minute Men——"

"Ethan!" Revere said. "Do you think it's wise to tell this young lady, who after all——"

"Is the daughter of a Tory," Polly finished for him.

Ethan smiled at her almost tenderly.

"If Polly had ever told even one of the many things I've told her," he said, "we'd all be hanged by now, Paul."

Paul Revere looked at Polly curiously.

"Would you mind telling me why you happen to feel this way about our cause, Miss Knowles?" he said.

"Because Ethan is for it," Polly said.

Revere smiled.

"My felicitations, Ethan," he said. "May the two of you be blessed with ten tall American sons!"

Ethan's face was hot with embarrassment.

"Come," he said gruffly, "we'd best be getting back now."

"No," Polly said, "let's ride through the streets for a while. I don't want to go back yet, Ethan . . ."

"If you don't mind," Revere said, "I'd better stay here. I have to at least pretend to make pots and pans for a while yet or even these stupid Britishers will be suspicious . . ."

Bless you for your tact, Polly thought.

" 'Night, Paul," Ethan said. "You know where to reach me . . ."

They rode very quietly through the streets without saying anything at all.

I won't talk to him unless he talks to me first, Polly thought. I simply won't!

They turned into a street near the Charles. Suddenly the door of a tavern opened and a horde of men poured out into the street. They were very big men, blond for the most part, red-faced, beefy. They were dressed in blue coats and white pantaloons. They were armed with bayonets, but no firearms.

They stopped still, gaping at Polly. Their little piglike eyes were bloodshot. Then they started to grin. "A maiden!" one of them roared. "Pretty, not so?"

"No. She has no fat. She is so small and thin . . ."

"But, she is a girl. Come on!"

"Who are they, Ethan?" Polly whispered. "What on earth are they talking about?"

"Hessians!" Ethan said grimly. "I don't know what they're saying, but I don't like it. Stay close to me."

They rode forward slowly.

The Germans moved out, blocking the street. They stood there, grinning.

Ethan put his hand in his saddlebags and came out with two big pistols. He cocked them one at a time, the noise sounding ominously through the silent street.

"*'Raus!*" he roared suddenly. "*'Raus mit dich, verdamnter schwein!*"

The Hessians stared at the big horse pistols. Then they broke and let Ethan and Polly through.

"Ride!" Ethan hissed. "Ride like the devil!"

Five blocks further they pulled up their horses.

"Ethan!" Polly laughed. "What did you say to them? What do those words mean?"

"Blessed if I know," Ethan grinned. "It's something their officers say. I've watched them drill dozens of times. I just happened to remember it. Thank God it worked . . ."

"Ethan," Polly said seriously, "why did they stop us? What would they have done?"

"Killed me," Ethan said bluntly. "Taken you."

"My God!" Polly whispered.

"Amen. Never get within a mile of a Hessian, Polly. The lobsterbacks have a pretty good record as far as women are concerned. Decent women are safe enough from them. But not those Hessian pigs."

"Take me back now, Ethan," Polly said. "I've had more than enough excitement for one night . . ."

"Me too. But I'm glad of those Hessians in a way . . ."

Polly stared at him.

"Why, Ethan?"

"Because they've swung so many lukewarm people, and even former Tories, over to our side. Many King's men admit that the Blockade of Boston is unjust. It hurts their business as well as ours. Where they differ from us is that they believe that King George can be brought to see the light, that matters can be corrected short of war, short of independence. But when a king looses foreign mercenaries on his own flesh and blood, men begin to lose patience. Men stop being King's men and become patriots. And since the Tory classes include some of the finest men and best brains in America, our recruits from their ranks are especially valuable—they tend to counteract our visionaries, our fire-eaters, and our wild men. . . ."

They rode in silence the rest of the way back to Peter Knowles' house. Ethan's thoughts were upon war and glory, but Polly's were much simpler:

I wish, she thought fervently, oh, how I wish he'd kiss me good night!

But he didn't. And Polly went upstairs, and cried herself to sleep. Again.

Many people saw the lanterns hanging in the tower of the North Church early on the night of April eighteenth. But Polly was one of the few who understood what they meant. She had seen the British officers pounding away on all the roads that led out of Boston. Now the lanterns swaying there and in other high places, she could only grip her hands and pray. Ethan would be riding tonight. Ethan and Paul Revere and four or five other messengers. She had no way of knowing that Ethan's ride would be forgotten, the others would be unknown after a year, and only little Paul, because he was lucky enough to draw the Lexington-Concord Road, would gallop into immortality.

Polly saw Ethan before he left. She saw him in the full and bitter knowledge that it was Kathy he sought, not her.

"Kathy?" he said.

"She's not here, Ethan," Polly said quietly.

"Where?" Ethan said.

"I don't know," Polly lied. She knew all too well. Kathy was out riding with Cecil Fitzgerald, the next Viscount Linkletter. The title intrigued Kathy. The splendid red uniform. Maybe even the man.

But she couldn't tell Ethan that now. Not with those beacons of death glowing in the church towers at scattered points throughout the city. Not when Ethan was going to ride out through roads filled with British soldiers, and at any moment . . .

She couldn't phrase the thought. Not even in the darkness of her mind.

"Sorry," Ethan mumbled.

Polly stood there with her two slim arms wrapped about her own body.

"Ethan——"

"Yes, Polly?"

"It's going to be bad, isn't it?"

"No, Polly—it's going to be glorious!"

It's only the men who talk about glory, Polly thought. They have it easy. All they have to do is to ride out—and die. A little puff of flame from a musket and some pain, maybe even bad pain but over in a little while, then the dark and the quiet. But they don't have to wait and die inside their bodies a thousand times and come alive with hope and die again with despair . . . I don't think they could do it, these little boys talking about glory and playing soldier.

But she didn't say that. What she said was:

"Take care of yourself, Ethan."

He grinned at her crookedly.

"I aim to," he said. Then he swung himself into the saddle. The horse's hoofs threw up little spurts of mud as he bounded off.

Polly stood there, clenching and unclenching her hands.

I should have made him kiss me, she thought. I should have made him kiss me good-by. . . .

Then she turned and went back into the house.

The route that Ethan had been assigned made a long loop northward out of Boston through Medford, Woburn, Bedford. At each town and at each house along the road, sleepy-eyed men tumbled out of bed to his gloved fist's pounding at their doors and stood there with their good wives behind them clad in nightcap and gown, holding the candle aloft above their husbands' heads so that they could peer into the face of the messenger.

"The British?" the men growled, and all the sleep went out of their eyes at once. "Right. Be ready in a minute."

And behind him all up that road they spewed out of their houses in rough clothes with musket or rifle or fowling piece gripped in their horny hands, and their wives stood behind them with tight faces, dry-eyed, and watched their men go. The women of America had not yet learned to cry.

Behind him, and behind the other messengers pounding through the other roads. Of them all, little Paul Revere made the most noise. Ethan and the other riders lacked his flair for the dramatic.

Ethan's ride ended in Bedford. That was as far as he had been told to go. But Bedford isn't very far from either Lexington or Concord. And if anything was going to happen, it was going to happen in one of those two places. The biggest cache of ammunition the patriots had was in Concord. And in Lexington, hidden in the house of the Rev. Jonas Clark, were Samuel Adams and John Hancock, whom the British were itching to hang.

Ethan sat on his horse and figured things out. That ammunition dump wasn't going to move. The British probably knew that they could get around to it at their leisure. But Hancock and Adams—as soon as little Paul got to them—were going to run like all the hounds of hades were after them. Even if fat Major Pitcairn of the Royal Infantry had not taken into consideration the possibility of their being warned, he'd still be more inclined to go after rebels with legs first, rather than powder and ball that had no legs.

So Ethan Page turned his horse's head toward Lexington. He was spoiling for a fight.

He reached Lexington at three o'clock in the morning of April nineteenth. Not a soul was in sight. All the brave patriots who had responded to the ringing of the church bells more than an hour before had left the field. It was just too dadblamed cold to stand out there on Lexington Green and wait for an enemy so slow in putting in his appearance. Some of them had gone home, kicked off their boots, and lay down beside their wives, fully dressed, with their flintlocks at easy reach. Some were poking around Lexington looking for some fun. The rest, Ethan found in the one true, indisputable cradle of American liberty, Buckman Tavern.

It was cold enough outside to freeze the hinges of hades, but the fat tavern keeper knew how to make rum flips, and his brandy was fire itself.

Ethan downed nearly a quart of it, in company with his rollicking fellows. They sang a good many songs. The words of these songs would have made Polly and Kathy run from the room, covering up their ears. One true patriot got up on the table and toasted King George. It took him a long time to do it because he climbed up and down poor George's family tree, making Ethan laugh 'til the tears ran down his cheeks.

They had been there for thirty minutes when Paul Revere clattered into town. Little Paul was terribly late. He had been so busy dashing about, shouting himself hoarse, that he got to Lexington long after somebody else—a local citizen, perhaps, who had seen the British officers galloping through the lanes—had warned the town. But Paul did do some good: he got Hancock and Adams out of bed at Rev. Clark's and sped them on their way. Ethan and the Minute Men, drinking Buckman's most patriotic brandy, had long since forgotten about them.

Just before dawn the bells rang again. All the patriots bundled themselves up and trooped out to the Green opposite the white Congregational Church. They stood there, looking at each other, and the cold air took some of the edge off that brandy. They looked at each other sheepishly and a little afraid and their mouths were dry. They would have liked very much to go back into Buckman's and imbibe a little more patriotism. They needed it. The cold was draining it out of them right down through their very toes.

Ethan remembered wondering if Julius Caesar's legions in Gaul, which he had read about at Harvard College, had ever felt half frozen and scared witless and a good bit hung over from drinking brandy in a tavern. Then he decided that human nature had probably changed very little over the centuries and that men—even men who had actually done heroic deeds, only began to feel like heroes years after the battles were over and they had forgotten the precise nature of events. So he stood there with his horse pistols in his hands and his toes aching from the cold and his head aching from the brandy and his mouth hot and dry despite the cold, and the whole of him shaking a little from anticipation and a great deal more from fear. He wished he could see Kathy right now, or even Polly, though he didn't care very much about her then. But most of all he wished he hadn't drunk so much brandy. At the moment he doubted that he could hit the side of a barn.

A moment later he was wishing it harder than ever, for the rolling of drums had come down the wind and above it fifes crying like all the amorous and combative tomcats in the world tossed into a single lane. Then the bright red regiments of the King's advance guard rounded a bend into sight, with fat Major Pitcairn riding at their head.

Ethan couldn't breathe. Every red-clad arm swung

in perfect unison with every other. The black boots thundered against the earth with a single sound. They came on, the fifes caterwauling, the red faces glaring a little at the ragged rabble blocking their path.

We can't beat them! Ethan thought. Those are soldiers!

The colonial militia didn't hold its formation. It hadn't had any formation to hold in the first place. The Minute Men strutted around, holding themselves up very stiffly. But no one of them broke and ran. That's all it would have taken, Ethan knew. Just one and the rest would have been flying at his heels, throwing away their muskets as they ran.

Then a British officer on a big black horse detached himself from the others. His regimentals sparkled in the morning sun. He came on, drawing his saber and waving it. He pointed it at Captain Parker.

"Lay down your arms!" he bellowed. "Disperse, you rebels!"

A lank and tattered militiaman spat half a quid of tobacco out of the side of his mouth. Then he lifted his musket and shot at the British officer. He missed him cleanly but the shot hit Major Pitcairn's mount in the flank, causing the beast to rear. If the Major hadn't been so fat, he would have been thrown off. Then somebody else shot a British soldier and another patriot put a ball in Pitcairn's mount's other flank.

That, Ethan grinned to himself, is the most perforated animal in the British Army!

He wasn't afraid any more. He felt very fine. The brandy curled warm in his stomach and even his feet weren't cold any more.

He didn't even notice that so far the British hadn't fired a single shot.

Fat Pitcairn was trying to control his rearing horse. "Surround 'em!" he roared.

The patriots were grinning and leveling their muskets. Some of them were having a hard time keeping them leveled.

But the young subaltern on the black horse was looking at the private with the musket ball through his shoulder. These farmers weren't playing games and he knew it.

"Fire on 'em!" he screamed out.

Ethan was surprised how quick it was over after that. One minute the whole world was blotted out by gun smoke with the tongues of flame spitting through it and the next minute the smoke lifted and there were men lying on the earth, all patriots and no redcoats, and the British were scattered all over the field and the farmers were shooting at them and cursing.

Ethan stood there, watching one of the men he'd been drinking with in the tavern an hour ago clawing the earth with his fingers and vomiting blood. His own stomach turned over inside of him and the cold sweat broke out on his forehead, but he held back the black waves of nausea.

Then all the militia fell back at once and the shooting stopped and the British closed ranks and marched on toward Concord. All the dogs for miles around were barking, and the women came streaming out of their houses still clad in their long white nightgowns and their frilly nightcaps, and threw themselves on the forms of husbands, sons, lovers, lying there on the blood-soaked grass and started screaming.

Ethan looked down at his own trembling hands and noticed that he still held both his pistols and that both of them were still cocked and neither of them had been fired.

"You," he said aloud, "are one hell of a soldier!"

Then he bent down and picked up the rifle that the dead man at his feet had dropped and joined the militiamen who were following the redcoats. They followed the British all the way into Concord, but they didn't fire a shot. They slunk from tree to tree like redskins, like shadows, and they waited.

Pitcairn took his lobsterbacks over the North Bridge into Concord. There he made a personal attack upon Jones' Tavern, kicking open the door and helping himself to Scotch whiskey with water on the side while his soldiers went about their work of wrecking the patriot arsenal.

It took them five hours. What they did was to spike two cannon, smash three barrels of flour, and throw five hundred pounds of ball in the river. Two husky bond servants could have done the same job in an hour. By that time fat Major Pitcairn was too drunk to lead his troops home, so even fatter Colonel Smith took command.

But when they got back to North Bridge they found four hundred ragged colonial militiamen standing there on the bridge and around it. The tall subaltern charged up to them and ordered them to disperse.

They didn't move. Standing there in the front ranks Ethan knew it wasn't brandy any more. It was something else, born of the memory of men clawing the grass at Lexington with their fingers and women screaming over the broken forms of their men.

Then behind the British right the cannon bucked and thundered and the air was alive with the whistle of grapeshot. Old Timothy Brown raised his musket, it smacked against his shoulder. A plump subaltern reeled out of line and lay on the ground crying. Like a woman. Like a child.

Ethan found himself firing, biting off cartridges, until his face was black as a Negro's, firing again. For six whole minutes this rabble in arms, these hayseeds, yokels, madmen, scum, pushed the British Army back into Concord. Then Colonels Buttrick and Davis ordered them to hold their fire. Men started to pick up the wounded.

Ethan saw the fat subaltern who was the first British soldier to fall. He was still alive, but not for long. For even as Ethan watched, a powder-blackened wild man with flaming eyes walked over to the wounded Britisher and sank a tomahawk into his brain. Then he knelt down and scalped him expertly, and straightened up with his bloody trophy in his hand.

He saw Ethan staring at him.

"My paw, and my brother," he said, "both. At Lexington this morning." Then he tied his dripping prize to his belt.

Ethan helped lift the wounded. He was shaking. But he had killed men himself, and between a tomahawk and a musket ball what were the odds? It wasn't sporting, but sportsmanship didn't win wars. . . .

Even too much concern with your own wounded didn't because if Buttrick and Davis had bottled the

British up in Concord, there wouldn't have been any redcoats left in an hour.

But Buttrick and Davis were gentlemen farmers, not soldiers, and they couldn't stand hearing their own wounded cry. So Colonel Smith got his terrified men back into rank and flew across the bridge. And when the Yankee farmers saw the redcoats flying away on the double, they broke ranks and flew after them, disobeying orders, leaving their officers to come pounding after them.

Then, unburdened by any trained or half-trained military man's conception of how the thing should be done, they fought the first, and perhaps the last, really intelligent battle of the entire war.

Ethan never forgot the lessons he learned that day. The business of war is to kill the enemy, not to stage pretty parades. These hayfoot, strawfoot yokels who couldn't keep step, didn't know a file from a rank or a squad from a platoon, but they knew what a tree was for, a rock was for, and a wall. . . .

It was as plain as the nose on your face. The idea was to kill as many lobsterbacks as possible while staying alive yourself. And Ethan reflected happily, There's something mighty comforting about a stout stone fence 'twixt you and the enemy's grapeshot and musketball. . . .

The British troops in their bright red coats were sitting ducks to these woodsmen. It wasn't nice. It was mean fighting, dirty fighting, without an ounce of sportsmanship in it. But Ethan was reorganizing his thinking. He came that morning to the startlingly simple conclusion that the nasty, stinking business of man-killing was hardly a game anyhow, and the only rules that applied were the ones that would get it over quickest, with the fewest dead on your side and the most corpses on the enemy's.

So he ran with the rest, and ducked behind trees, and shot from behind boulders, behind walls, out of farmhouse windows, from anywhere, in fact, that the British hadn't a ghost of a chance of hitting him while he had every chance in the world of hitting them.

There wouldn't have been any British troops left out of that company if Earl Percy hadn't come riding up on his white charger with re-enforcements. The patriots numbered thousands now, because nothing succeeds like success. The most arrant cowards in the countryside were out taking pot shots once they learned that the lobsterbacks were on the run. . . .

That was another advantage of bushwhacking, Ethan learned. A coward was just as valuable as a hero when you put a stone wall in front of him to stop the enemy's bullets.

More valuable, he told himself, grinning with his white teeth gleaming in his powder-blackened face, 'cause there're always a heck of a lot more of them. . . .

All Percy could do was to slow the rout. The colonials chased his fresh troops along with Smith's beaten ones clear back to Charlestown, where nightfall ended the battle. Then they turned and marched into Cambridge, and encamped there, leaving on that cool green road between Concord and Charlestown 273 of the King's finest sprawled out in those grotesque positions that can never be counterfeited in life. . . .

There could be no turning back now, Ethan knew. This was war . . . .

CHAPTER 4

Boston was the only place in America now where it was reasonably safe to be a loyalist. In every town and hamlet from Maine to Georgia where there weren't any British soldiers to protect them, King's men and their families were beaten, tarred and feathered, their homes ransacked. Sometimes they were forced to kneel in the street and recant.

But in Boston it was different. In Boston, Polly Knowles could take a ride out in the countryside and not even be stopped by the sentries because at one time or another practically every British officer of importance had been entertained at the Knowles' house. To gain this privilege, all she had had to do was to say to Cecil Fitzgerald:

"I don't like being cooped up in the city. I want to see the wild flowers bloom . . ."

And Cecil, being by this time head over heels in love with Kathy, would do anything to indulge her younger sister—even to instructing the sentries on the major roads that Miss Knowles was not to be halted or subjected to any inconvenience or he'd have their hides . . .

The only wild flower that Polly was remotely interested in seeing certainly wasn't blooming. He was sitting outside of his little tent at Cambridge, and growling at the world in general simply because he was bored to tears.

For weeks now men had been pouring into Cambridge. They came down from their rocky farms with rusty flintlocks, smoothbores, seven-foot-long rifles, which were the only guns made that could hit what they were aimed at, all varieties of pistols, and ancient fowling pieces with belled muzzles, looking for all the world like trumpets. They could make their own ball, and they could steal powder from the British.

Only the British were staying in Boston and wouldn't come out and fight. They had an understandable reluctance to face a foe who killed them from concealment, and who had so little respect for the rules of gentlemanly warfare.

But the waiting at Cambridge was playing hob with morale. Fat old General Artemas Ward had a chronic belly-ache, so that he had to hold his big stomach with his hands as he rode among his troops. The ragged troops hooted at him, got drunk and staged fist fights over cards, and wasted ammunition shooting at robins for want of any redcoats. There was one Captain to every three privates. And the privates were quite capable of telling their officers where to go when given an order they didn't like—such as learning to drill in the warm June sun. There was no organization. No sentries. If the British Army had for once decided to march quietly into Cambridge without their infernal fifes and drums, they would have found the whole American force asleep, or drunk, or playing cards.

Which was precisely how Polly Knowles found them when she rode into camp to pay Ethan a visit. Her coming caused quite a commotion. She was escorted up to Ethan's tent by two dozen sweaty, grinning rebels.

"Lookee, Eth!" they laughed. "Look what we brung you!"

"Come on, Eth boy—give her a buss! Lord, she's pretty. Missy, you got any sisters or cousins, maybe? I ain't seen a pretty woman in so blamed long . . ."

Ethan stood up, smiling.

"Off with you, you blackguards," he roared in wrath, "the young lady and I have to plan how to win this war . . ."

"Board o' strategy, eh? But Eth, by the time you done finished yore planning we're gonna have used up all the redcoats—'lessen you ask us to save 'em a few real kindly like . . ."

Polly's face was red as a sunset, but in spite of herself she had to smile. She liked these rebels. They hadn't any manners, their clothes were in tatters, and they didn't smell nice, but they were fun.

They hadn't the faintest intention, however, of leaving her alone with Ethan. Most of them were squatting on the ground like Indians in a semicircle around the tent, staring at her in frank and unabashed admiration.

"Tell me, missy," one of them said, "what do ye see in old Eth? He's as skinny as a rail fence, and he shore ain't pretty. Now take me, fer instance . . ."

"Take you!" his comrades hooted. "Why the first time your maw looked into the crib, she sung out to yore paw: 'Come here, Ely, for God's sake—there be a b'ar in the baby's bed!' "

Polly laughed so hard that the tears streaked her face.

Attracted by the laughter, an officer rode up. He

had a big head and bigger shoulders. The muscles of his arms seemed about to burst through his rumpled uniform. Seeing Polly sitting there before the tent, he doffed his hat and got down from his horse. His hair was gray, and he was just about the ugliest man that Polly had ever seen.

"Who might this be, Eth?" he bellowed. Afterwards, Polly discovered that a bellow was his normal tone of voice.

"Miss Polly Knowles," Ethan said. "Polly, may I present General Israel Putnam?"

Polly rose and dropped old Put a very pretty curtsy.

"Damme, Eth!" General Putnam roared. "I crave the privilege of kissing yore lady's hand!"

Ethan grinned.

"And if I refuse, sir?" he said.

"Court-martial, by thunder! Penalty, death by hanging—and afore I have 'em drag you out, I'm gonna see that you leave me this young lady in yore will!"

Polly got up again, pure mischief in her brown eyes. She walked over to old Put and caught the lapels of his uniform in her two hands. Then she kissed him three times, once on the right cheek, once on the left, then full on the mouth. All the soldiers stood up and cheered.

Old Put turned beet red.

"Eth," he roared, "stand up!"

Ethan stood up.

"I hereby appoint you Colonel Ethan Page, for meritorious services to yore country in her hour of need!"

The troops yelled like Indians, and fired off their guns in the air.

"And you have my permission, Colonel," General

Putnam grinned, "to take yore lady for a nice long ride where they ain't no prying eyes about. Git along with you now!"

"Yes, sir!" Ethan saluted. "Thank you, sir."

"Don't thank me," old Put growled. "Thank yore lady. That were the sweetest commission I ever give out!"

"You know," Polly said, as they rode away from the camp, "I think he means it about making you a Colonel."

"He does," Ethan said. "He has the right to commission officers in the field. In fact, in the present state of disorganization of the Army, that's the only way it can be done. He had already promised me a commission, logically enough, Polly, because so few of us have any education—and even to be able to read and write makes a man officer material. But I'm sure that he jumped me a couple of grades because you kissed him. I'd expected to be made a Lieutenant—at most a Captain. Many thanks, Polly . . ."

Under the trees in the woodland, it was very quiet. The sunlight sifted through the leaves in patches, and here and there in crannies in the stone walls, and in the grass along the roadside, the wild flowers were blooming. It was peaceful. Polly had a hard time remembering that men died along these roads, clutching at their torn bellies in agony, and clawing this green and pleasant earth.

And that more would die. Maybe even—Ethan.

She didn't like to think that. There were so many things she had to accomplish. She was almost sure that Ethan had lost Kathy—that her sister was not going to let Cecil's handsome face, his splendid uniform, or his high-sounding title slip through her fingers. Kathy didn't understand what Ethan meant when he said "The People." Kathy would have been revolted by the actions of those soldiers Polly had just met in camp.

It was all a matter of taste—or was it? A difference in the heart, maybe. A difference at the root of the soul.

I am an American, Polly thought. Eth and I are the same kind. We can love people—even people who don't wash and who talk badly. They're God's children, too; and He must love them best—because He made so many of them. Maybe, after all this is over we'll have a country where everybody can dress well and learn to talk nicely. ...

But she wasn't sure she wanted that. She'd liked them so much the way they were: simple and fine and full of fun. But one thing troubled her.

"Ethan," she said, "How can we win? How can those poor simple fellows whip the British Army?"

Ethan smiled at her.

"God bless you for that 'we,' Pol," he said. "And don't worry about those fellows. They're the finest fighters in the whole dadblamed world. Half those boys around my tent were with me at Lexington and Concord. And look what Allen and his Green Mountain Boys and Benedict Arnold did at Fort Ticonderoga in May ... Remember one thing, Polly, the British Army hasn't won a battle from us yet—not one solitary battle...."

They rode on through the dappled sunlight. Polly could see Ethan looking at her out of the corner of his eye. She knew what he wanted to know, but by now his respect for her was so great that he didn't want to hurt her by asking. So she told him anyhow—not the truth, but what he wanted most of all to hear.

"Kathy's fine," she said firmly. "She sent you her love."

She lied in her teeth and she knew it. But Polly had sound womanly instincts about those things. She knew that if Ethan ever discovered the truth about Kathy, his knowledge would have to come from another source. Men never quite forgive the bearers of such ill tidings. And more, having found out for himself, he could not help but have increased admiration for the possessor of such information who refused to use it to her own advantage.

But it was hard to ride through the wooded lanes with him like this, knowing that all that stood between them now were phantoms and shadows—the ghost of a love that had ceased to be.

Kathy never really loved him, Polly thought bitterly, not like I do—never like I do. . . .

Looking at him now, the bitter images of all the things her sister was doing ran through her mind: Kathy riding with young Cecil, singing love songs with him at the spinet, dancing with him—even disappearing with him for long hours at a time, and openly defying their mother's expressed commands.

But I can't quarrel with that, can I? Polly thought. I disappear with Ethan every chance I get. Kathy's far too smart for that. She knows how to tease a man until he'll come to her on her terms. . . .

She looked at Ethan and her face was filled with adoration.

No, she mused, 'tis I who am the foolish one. I

have too much heart and too little sense. Oh Ethan, don't you know? Can't you see that you need only to stretch out your arms to me and I'd fly into them?

She turned her face away from him suddenly, so suddenly that Ethan saw the gesture. He looked at her sadly.

Poor little Polly, he thought. I wish I could forget Kathy—I only wish I could!

As though she could read his mind, Polly turned back toward him.

"Don't pity me, Ethan," she said. "Don't you dare!"

The British were landing thousands of troops in Boston. The *Cerberus* had brought over three fine generals: Sir Henry Clinton, Sir William Howe, and John Burgoyne, who was also a playwright. Some of the officers brought their families with them. And some of the officers and their families and hundreds of the soldiers died en route from bad food and scurvy, and smallpox.

To Polly, seeing them land, they looked rather pitiful. They were wrung white from seasickness and storms at sea and vile food and crowding below deck in abominable quarters.

But they recovered quickly enough, and got to be quite cocky because none of them had been on that road between Concord and Cambridge, so they didn't know what they were up against. Some of the officers acquired themselves pretty Tory sweethearts and learned to drink arrack and applejack. In loyalist circles, the town was ablaze with parties.

But even the Tories fell silent when they saw the big Hessians marching through the streets. That was a hard thing to stomach. Soldiers in anybody's army aren't noted for overly nice manners, but the redcoats were well disciplined and committed few offences against the populace. The Hessians were another matter. Every day the Knowles' household heard new tales of their brutality. There were other tales, too, told in whispers. All these stories were grossly exaggerated. The only trouble was, Polly soon discovered, that these stories had a hard core of truth at their heart.

She couldn't ride out to see Ethan now. It was far too dangerous. In one way, that was a relief. She didn't have to evade her mother's angry scoldings for a kind of behavior that to Gertrude was simply unmaidenly, or her uncle's persistent questions as to where she had been. At that, she had been lucky. Uncle Peter was not so strong a character as her father. Polly knew well that her quiet but open defiance of her mother's and her uncle's commands would have been impossible at home. But Uncle Peter was so busy that he couldn't keep up with her comings and goings; and her mother, troubled about both Polly and Kathy, was too ashamed of her willful daughters to bring it to her brother-in-law's attention. As far as Polly was concerned, Gertrude's anxiety was confined to the appearance of things, what the neighbors would think, and nothing more. She well knew Polly's sound sense of values. But she worried more about her frivolous and impressionable Kathy.

But Polly had her own problems: her health suffered. She hardly slept any more. She was down to skin and bones from lack of interest in food. Seeing the precise, perfect formations of the King's Army drilling on the Common, she feared for Ethan's life. She reached the state where she seldom spoke to Kathy or her mother for days at a time. She didn't want to talk to Kathy, or even be near her sister. She was afraid of what she might say. Not out of jealousy, but because Kathy was so happy and gay with these redcoats who would willingly kill all those who fought for liberty.

In her heart, she recognized the fact that she was being unjust to Kathy. Her sister hadn't changed. She had always been gay, thoughtless, fickle, vain. But she had always been kind and affectionate toward Polly, too. She still was. No, Polly thought, 'tis I who have changed. I am in love with a man who doesn't want me. And I have almost lost my family's love. It's true that I believe in liberty and the things that Ethan is fighting for; but would I suffer all this for them, were it not for him? Yet, I can't help it—I can't help it at all!

The voices woke her that morning of June seventeenth. She heard Susie Lawrence and Kathy and the servants talking excitedly up on the roof over her head.

"It's a fort!" Kathy said. "Oh, Susie, they've built a fort! Now Peyton and Cecil will have to attack them! Oh, Sue, I'm afraid!"

Polly ran up the spiral stairs that led to the cupola on the roof, without even bothering to throw a robe over her nightdress.

"Where is it?" she cried. "Where's this fort?"

"Over there, Polly," Kathy said, and pointed, "across the Charles just behind Charlestown. Don't you see? It's up on top of Bunker Hill."

"That ain't Bunker Hill, missy," a servant corrected

her. "That's Breed's Hill. That there's Bunker Hill a little more to the west. . . ."

Polly saw the pitiful little rampart atop Breed's Hill. From talking with Ethan she'd learned a great many military terms. That single wall of earth built against a rail fence was nobody's fort. It was simply a redoubt. At one glance, Polly, who had never been trained in military tactics and who was therefore incapable of making the tomfool mistakes as natural to the military mind as breathing, saw how absolutely untenable that redoubt was.

They had built it on Breed's Hill out on the end of the peninsula. All those British men-of-war lying in the harbor had to do was to send a few boatloads of marines to land on the neck of the peninsula behind Breed's Hill and march quietly up and slaughter the patriots whose earthen wall protected them only in front, leaving their ragged backsides at the mercy of any fire from the landward side.

Fools! Fools! Hadn't they seen that? Now Ethan was going to die. He was up there. Polly was sure of that. Ethan Page was always anywhere there was going to be a fight. Only this wasn't going to be a fight. This was going to be slaughter—suicide.

She put down her head and began to pray very hard. But she hadn't gotten any further than, "Please, Dear God——" when the British warships in the harbor opened up.

She shook under the impact of the cannonading. The slow rolling thunder tore into her. She put her hand in her mouth and bit it to keep from screaming.

They were shooting at Ethan.

She could see the cannon balls skipping along the

grass. Most of them hit far short of the redoubt. A few hit it. But the earth stopped them.

Not that way, Polly thought, they won't be able to shell them out of there. It'll take bayonets. . . .

She hung there, trembling. She never should have thought of bayonets. She was sick all over. She wanted to retch. She shut her eyes, but even with them shut she remembered what a British bayonet looked like— two feet of needle-pointed steel slashing . . .

Dear God, would they never finish shooting?

They kept it up for hours. Long before it was over, Kathy and Susie led her downstairs, helped her to dress, poured some brandy into her.

Kathy looked at her younger sister with tears in her violet eyes.

"It's Ethan, isn't it, Polly?" she whispered. "You're worried about Ethan?"

Polly couldn't talk. All she could do was to nod her head.

"And there's Cecil on the other side," Kathy wept, "and Peyton, too. I—I love Cecil, Polly . . ."

"I know," Polly said.

"Oh, Polly, how awful!" Kathy wailed, and fell into her sister's arms.

Polly stroked her bright hair gently.

"Don't cry, Kathy," she said. "There's nothing to cry over—yet . . . Maybe neither of them——"

"Polly!" Kathy got out. "Suppose—suppose they meet—up there on that hill—Ethan and Cecil, I mean . . . I'm terribly fond of Ethan. I would have married him if—if all this hadn't happened . . . But suppose Ethan and Cecil meet!"

"Or Ethan and Peyton," Susie Lawrence put in bleakly.

"God forbid," Polly said.

They couldn't hear the guns any more, so they went back to the roof. They didn't want to go, but they had to. Staying downstairs, not knowing, was just too awful.

Polly saw the boats start out from the British men-of-war. The oars stroked, lifted, flashing in the sun. They were packed with soldiers. The sun was very bright. The soldiers' red coats were the color of blood against the blue water.

From the landward side, too, from Boston, they began to push out over the Charles River.

Still no sign of life from the top of Breed's Hill.

From the top of a neighboring house other women laughed and waved handkerchiefs. Polly could feel the rage boiling through her veins. She wanted to kill those women. What did they think this was—a picnic?

Apparently most of Boston did think just that. The rooftops were crowded with citizenry, patriots and Tories alike, cheering, waving scarves, handkerchiefs.

Down there at the foot of Breed's Hill, the drums were rolling, now. The red-coated soldiers fell into ranks.

"Oh, heavens!" Polly gasped. "They're going to attack from the front! I wonder why they're doing that? Can't they see that the Colonials will slaughter them?"

She felt a great rush of pity for those nice English boys marching under their banners to the sound of fife and drum up Breed's Hill into the mouths of the rebel muskets. Sir William Howe had to prove something. He had to prove that the British soldiers were the bravest men alive, that no band of cowherds could stand against them. But, Polly thought, what's the good of being brave when you're dead?

On top of Breed's Hill, Ethan Page looked long and hard in the direction of the Knowles' house. He couldn't make it out, among all the other houses, but he kept looking.

I wonder if Polly has a glass, he thought, so she can see me die?

Then it came to him that he had said Polly, not Kathy, and the thought startled him. Guess it's because I know Polly cares, he thought bitterly, and Kathy'll wipe her eyes and go dancing with a lobsterback to-morrow night. . . .

"There aren't any Yankees up there," the British laughed. "Show yourselves, you rebel dogs! Yellow-bellied farmers—put up your blinking 'eads so a sol-dier of the King can blast 'em off!"

They started to sing "Hot Stuff," their favorite song. They came on boldly, carelessly.

General Israel Putnam shifted his quid of tobacco from his right cheek to his left.

"Hold yer fire," he called out. "Wait 'til you see the whites of their eyes. Then up with ye lads, and tear out their bellies! Shoot for the belt, damn 'em!"

At Ethan's side a tall Connecticut Yankee stood up.

"Colonel Abercombie!" he twanged. "Oh, Colonel Abercombie, d'you think we Yankees are cowards?"

Colonel Abercombie lifted his sword over his head, and his Twenty-Second Grenadiers came foaming up the hill on the double. Off to his left young Peyton Cranbrooke saw the Grenadiers break into a trot and spurred on his own company of Royal Marines.

Fifteen yards now. Ten.

"Up and at 'em, boys!" old Put thundered.

Ethan and men around him lunged upward, atop that wall. The whole world dissolved into musket smoke shot through with flame. Sound went away from their ears, blasted deaf with gunfire.

On the housetops of Boston, people stopped cheering.

The smoke of the musketry lifted. The British were pounding down the slope. Some of the British. In front of that redoubt, the bodies of the rest of them were piled up like cordwood.

Polly turned just in time to catch Susie Lawrence as she pitched forward in a dead faint. She eased her down to the roof. Then she stood up and left her there. Plenty of time later to attend to fainting females. Out there on Breed's Hill there was no time left, no time at all.

Ethan could see General William Howe trying to rally his men. The General's white stockings were splashed with the blood of his men. Even with sickening bits of flesh. Because the British at Concord had destroyed most of the patriots' musket balls. So now at Breed's Hill they were firing nails, slag, bits of broken iron, stones—anything that would go down the muzzle of a musket. And what that broken rubble did to a man when it hit him was a sight to marvel at. Some of the dead Britishers down there in front of the redoubt had holes in them a man could ram his closed fist into.

Howe's voice came over to them through the stillness. His speech was very precise. Ethan wondered if Johnny Burgoyne, the playwright-General, had written them. They didn't sound like the kind of thing a man would say in the heat of battle.

"I shall not desire any one of you," the General said, "to advance one step beyond where I am at the head of your line. Up with you, lads—God Save the King!"

They came on again. Ethan felt a little sick, waiting for them. At Concord, on that road, they had killed them one at a time, running them to earth like foxes. But this was mass slaughter. This was butchery and as ugly as butchery—no, uglier.

At fifteen yards they blasted the front ranks into the earth.

Out of that first line, not one man in three escaped. They followed old Put's orders and shot at their bellies. They hadn't the ammunition to waste by aiming at their heads. But a man shot in the belly often doesn't die at once, and afterwards they could hear them crying. It wasn't a good sound to hear.

Behind Ethan, Will Clayton, the best marksman in the company, climbed up on a stone. He started shooting, lifting his seven-foot rifle that was one of the most accurate guns ever invented, and each time he fired a British officer went down on the blood-soaked earth and lay there without moving. Each time he fired he passed his rifle down and the men behind the redoubt handed him a freshly loaded one. Will fired twenty times, and killed twenty British officers,[1] while an entire company of Grenadiers leveled their muskets at him and loosed five full volleys before they brought him down.

[1]This is a matter of actual record.

Now, Ethan knew, was the time to retreat. They had almost no powder left, and precious little ball. He looked at old Put. But the old man was hanging on grimly. Ethan didn't want to die. He wanted most ardently to live. He thought about breaking and running for it. But he couldn't. Something had gone out from man to man behind that smashed and shot-torn wall of earth atop Breed's Hill. Ethan couldn't exactly put it into words, but it was something very fine. There weren't any words for it really. It was just that every man of that ragged, tattered, smoke-blackened crew was prepared to die in his tracks before he'd give up one more inch of American soil or leave his fellows.

Across the Charles, on her rooftop, Polly felt it. She was suddenly very calm. She had the feeling that if Ethan were going to die it would be good that he could die like that, very well and bravely. Everybody had to die. And if she had to lose him, it would be better to lose him like this, feeling proud of him, knowing that a new nation under God would be born of his blood and generations of men and women as yet unborn would stand up tall in liberty because of him.

Besides, it had just come to her that she wouldn't have to grieve out her life for him. Sin or no sin, nothing said she had to go on living with Ethan gone. She contemplated the idea calmly and she found it comforting.

The few British officers that were left held a conference. This time they sent their men up the hill in columns instead of in waves. The patriots had passed all their powder over to the few trained marksmen. The rest of them waited with bayonets fixed.

The redcoats came over the top. There was no ammunition left to stop them.

Ethan came up, and rammed his bayonet through the belly of a Grenadier. He yanked it out and the hot wetness splattered his own shirt. He broke the blow of a musket butt with the barrel of his rifle held crosswise and bayoneted the man who had aimed the blow a second later. Afterwards he couldn't remember it all. The human brain closes itself off from horror. He remembered seeing boys of fourteen standing there beside their grandsires throwing stones and pieces of iron until they were hacked to bits by the sabers of the British officers and even then lying on the earth, they continued to throw things until they died.

Ethan was crying, his tears making white tracks through the powder soot on his face. He was screaming curses that he didn't even hear, falling back slashing with his bayonet, bleeding from saber cuts and small bayonet pricks, fighting like a wounded she-bear with cubs or a cornered cougar.

He felt a heavy hand on his shoulder and saw old Put.

"Eth, boy," Israel Putnam bellowed, "let's get outa here. We been heroes enough for one day!"

Then the two of them turned and ran down the hill with the rest and the British sent a terrible cross fire through their ranks and littered the back slopes of Breed's Hill with the bodies of men in tattered, smoke-blackened, civilian dress. Ethan felt something slam against him but he kept running. Old Put ran like a boy in his teens.

What saved them was that Sir William Howe's gentlemanly stomach couldn't take any more. He called a halt despite Clinton's urging. So Ethan and the rest got back to Cambridge, seeing the smoke hovering over Charlestown, which the British had burned to the ground. And it wasn't until he got there that Ethan discovered that he had a musket ball through his shoulder.

The battle hadn't been over an hour when a young woman in a green riding habit rode up the slope of Breed's Hill. The British burial detail stared at her in astonishment, but they made no move to stop her. They were far too stunned at the size of the job before them. Out of Howe's total force of thirty-five hundred men, more than one thousand were dead on Breed's bloody slopes.

Polly didn't look at the red-coated bodies. She wasn't concerned about them. If a burial squad hadn't crossed her path with the body of young Peyton Cranbrooke, she wouldn't have known about him. She was sorry they did. She hated to have to tell Susie.

But on the other side, she did look at the dead. Nobody had come out to bury them yet. Polly looked at them and she didn't get sick or faint or do any of the things that a well-bred young lady might have been expected to. She studied their faces very carefully, trying to recognize them through the powder soot and the blood and the contortions of agony. Every time she came to a tall, slim body with black hair, she gripped the butt of the little pistol she had taken from the drawer of her uncle's secretary very tightly and every time she saw it wasn't Ethan, she loosened her grip.

Only, she couldn't really be sure. Some of them hadn't any faces. It wasn't until the next day, when she remembered how they looked, that she finally did get sick. Now she hadn't time. She had to know.

She gave it up finally, and rode on into Cambridge. She rode past the lines of dirty, stinking, exhausted men lying on the ground. Some of them leaned on their elbows and grinned at her.

"Give us a kiss, honey," they called. "We got whupped, but you ought to see them lobsterbacks!"

She rode straight over to Ethan's tent. He was sitting there before it on a little stool, and the surgeon was probing for the musket ball. There were irons heating in a fire to cauterize the wound. Ethan had a bottle of brandy, and every time the surgeon dug into his shoulder he took a drink and the sweat popped out on him. But he didn't make a sound.

Polly threw herself down from her mare.

"Ethan," she sobbed. "Oh Ethan, Ethan. . . ."

Ethan stood up and put his good arm around her. The blood and sweat and powder soot ruined her habit but she didn't care. She clung to him so that the pistol in her pocket was hard against him.

Ethan put his hand down and drew it out.

"What in thunder were you going to do with this?" he said.

Then he saw her eyes.

"My God," he whispered. Then he drew back his good arm and threw the little pistol into the underbrush beyond the tent.

"Never love anybody like that, Polly," he whispered. "No man is worth it."

"You are," Polly said.

"Sit down, dagnab it!" the surgeon said. "This ain't no trifling wound, boy. 'Sides, I got others to 'tend to."

Ethan sat down. Polly stood beside him and held the brandy bottle to his lips. It was empty by the time the surgeon straightened up.

"Got it, by God!" he said with some satisfaction.

"Maybe you better run along, young lady. This part ain't pretty."

"Yes, Polly," Ethan groaned. "I might yell. This is going to be bad."

"No," Polly said. "Get up a minute."

Ethan got up and she sat down on the stool. Then she drew him down and put his head in her lap, hiding his face in the folds of her skirt.

But Ethan didn't yell, not even when the surgeon seared the wound with his red-hot irons. He merely fainted very quietly.

And Polly sat there a long time, stroking his wet black hair with her soft and gentle hands.

CHAPTER 5

It was necessary, Colonel Ethan Page found, to spruce the men under his command up a bit. They had to be made to look somewhat like soldiers. They had to learn to drill in close formation. For the life of him, Ethan couldn't see what difference it made what they looked like, or if they could drill at all as long as they could lick the tar out of the British. And that they had proved they could do.

But orders were orders—especially when they came from the Commander in Chief. So Ethan got a supply of needles and thread from Polly, and rounded up his crew of villainous-looking backwoodsmen. He had them all sitting around his tent mending their torn garments. His own campstool had become a barber's chair and Ethan himself was shaving his men one at a time and clipping their hair. Polly stood by with a supply of black ribbons to tie their pigtails with, and a barrel of flour to powder their hair. She had even brought a mirror along so that they could see what they looked like.

It was this mirror that caused all the trouble. Nobody wanted to give it up to the next man. Each of them stood there staring into it, swearing:

"By heaven, I'm fine! Never knowed I was so gosh-blamed pretty!"

Then the next man would snatch it away. They were

very good-natured about it, and their scuffles about the mirror were plain horseplay, but they made a lot of noise.

The next thing Ethan knew the Commander in Chief was glaring down at them from atop his big white horse.

"Who's in charge here?" he growled.

"I am, sir," Ethan said, and saluted.

"You are!" General Washington got out. "Then what the devil are you doing shaving these men?"

"Kind of thought they needed it, sir," Ethan said.

"That is beyond the question," the General snapped, "and a good bath as well. What's your rank, soldier?"

"Colonel, sir," Ethan said, "by General Putnam's appointment."

"Name?"

"Page, sir—Ethan Page."

"Don't I know your father?" George Washington said. "You aren't Daniel Page's son, are you?"

"Yes, sir," Ethan said.

The General's manner softened visibly.

"Colonel Page," he said sternly, "this fraternization between officers and enlisted personnel has got to stop. Bad for morale. From now on, your men are to address you with the respect due an officer. As I rode up, I heard one or two of them address you by your first name. Any of them who does that in the future must be reported for disciplinary action! Do I make myself clear?"

"Yes, sir!"

"Another thing, Colonel, the next time I see you, I want to see you attired in proper regimentals. It's impossible for us to uniform the men yet, but I expect my officers to look like soldiers. You can order one of the men to act as barber—that's beneath the dignity of an officer."

"Yes, sir," Ethan said. "I was going to, sir, but none of them know how . . ."

"That doesn't matter," George Washington thundered. "They can learn."

Ethan brought his right hand up in a salute. It's a good thing that was my left shoulder, he thought. I'd be in a fix if I couldn't salute this old martinet. . . .

General Washington returned the salute. As he did so, his gaze fell on Polly, standing by the flour barrel.

His gray eyes sparkled. George Washington had a Virginian's appreciation for horseflesh and pretty women.

"You might present me to the young lady, Colonel," he said.

"Yes, sir. General Washington, may I present Miss Polly Knowles?"

The General swung down from the big white horse. He swept off his hat and bowed over Polly's hand. Polly didn't even curtsy.

"Mighty pleased to make your acquaintance, ma'am," George Washington said.

"I'm not," Polly snapped. "I think you're a very mean man!"

George Washington straightened up and stared at her. Then he started to laugh. It was good laughter, big and booming and sincere. In spite of herself, Polly had to smile.

"My apologies, Miss Knowles," the General said. "I sometimes am. That's one of the bad parts about

being a General. It's like being a father. You sometimes do have to chastise your children . . ."

"Not for being nice to each other," Polly said. "Not
for helping each other out . . ."

"Polly, you don't understand," Ethan protested.

"The young lady is your intended?" General Washington asked.

"No, sir—I mean, sir—that things haven't gotten
that far along, yet . . ."

"Then see that they do," George Washington smiled.
"That's an order, Colonel! And Miss Knowles, I'd be
honored if you and the Colonel would join me at a
little party at headquarters tonight . . ."

"We'll be there, sir," Ethan said. "But, General, sir,
I won't be able to get a uniform by then . . ."

"I'll excuse you," the General said, "on condition
that Miss Knowles saves a dance for the mean man
. . ."

"Are you a good dancer, sir?" Polly asked mischiev-
ously.

"I've been told that I am," George Washington said.
"Why don't you come and see?"

He was, too, Polly discovered. He was an even better dancer than Ethan, and Ethan was good. One
young Captain was also invited, in order, Polly
guessed, that he might bring pretty little Mary Blaine,
his fiancée. General Washington delighted in having
handsome young women about him. He was always
the soul of courtesy to them, but it pleased him to
flirt and dance with them. Besides Polly and Mary
Blaine, there were Mrs. Henry Knox, Mrs. Horatio
Gates, and Mrs. Nathanael Greene . . .

The General was already beginning to write imploring letters to his own plump Martha, begging her to join him. He wasn't in love with Martha; his heart belonged forever to his lost Sally Fairfax, but he needed Martha. She was very bright and cheerful, without a jealous bone in her body, and she was very good for the General. Better, Polly afterwards always believed, than Sally ever could have been. Passionate love doesn't always help the relationship between a man and a woman—calm, goodhearted, friendly devotion like Martha's is sometimes better. . . .

That evening, Polly revised her opinion of the General.

"He's a good man," she told Ethan. "Of course, he's terribly stupid when it comes to people but his heart is good. I feel so sorry for him. He's got so much on his shoulders. No wonder he was cross today. . . ."

Ethan had a lot on his own shoulders. He couldn't get the memory of Breed's Hill out of his mind. The smell of blood and death stayed in his nostrils. He didn't seem to be changed, but he was. He was quieter, much more serious.

Polly didn't know it, but a new rival had almost displaced Kathy in Ethan's affections. He had a new sweetheart that rode with him night and day. Her name was—death.

I could marry Polly, he told himself. It's a matter of sound common sense. Kathy's terribly fickle. She's even against the cause (but she's lovely—dear God, but she's lovely!). Polly would never betray me. She'd die for me—and it's hard to shun devotion like that. I can't even see Kathy now, and Polly always comes to bring me things, wine and cakes and stockings.

She's sweet and she's good and she's getting prettier every day . . .

That's the rub. She's too sweet, too good. What right have I to tie her life to mine? There would be children. I can't. I can't bind her to me, and then leave her. I can't march out to fight knowing that dying, I'd leave her in want with other hungry mouths to feed. Wouldn't be much of a fighter then. I'd betray the cause, betray myself. A man's no soldier who dares not die . . .

Polly stretched out her hand and took his.

"Don't think like that, Ethan," she said.

Ethan stared at her.

"I really think you can read my mind," he said.

"No, but I always know when you're thinking unhappy thoughts. Your face shows it. You—you were thinking about Kathy—weren't you?"

"No," Ethan said, "I was thinking about you."

"What were you thinking, Ethan?"

"How easy it would be to let myself love you," Ethan said honestly, "and how wrong . . ."

"Wrong?" Polly said. "Oh, Ethan, how . . ."

"Listen to me, little Polly. You saw Breed's Hill. You know how much chance I or any of us here— have of coming out of this alive?"

"I know," Polly said calmly. "Practically none."

"Then you understand how wrong it would be for me to link my life to yours. My life isn't my own, Polly. It belongs to my country—to the country we're trying to make. I've got to be free—to die if need be, without hesitation—without having to wonder how my infant sons will fare without me. You see that, don't you, Polly?"

"General Washington has Martha," Polly said. "General Knox has Lucy. Nathanael Greene has his Catharine. And their risk is the same as yours . . ."

"They had their wives before," Ethan said. "They didn't marry them in the certainty of making widows of them!"

Polly looked away from him toward where George Washington was dancing with Lucy Knox to the tune of the fiddles.

"I shouldn't like to be your widow," she whispered. "I can't think of anything I'd like less. But I'd rather be your widow than have been nothing to you at all . . ."

She turned upon him suddenly, fiercely, gripping the lapels of his coat with her two hands.

"Oh Ethan, Ethan, can't you see? You talk about dying—but that's an easy thing compared to this! Maybe it's not right, but when you mouth your noble sentiments about not tying my life to yours all you do is to make me go on dying by slow inches from wanting you . . ."

"Polly!"

"Shocked you, didn't I? I'm glad. I mean to go on shocking you until I shock some sense into your head. You talk about how our infant sons would fare—funny, I always think of them as daughters—that's none of your business, Ethan. They'd fare all right, because being yours they'd be strong and brave and beautiful like you; and being mine they'd be tough and sensible. You haven't any right to deny me that. For, having them, I'd have something left, and now you propose to march away and leave me nothing of you—nothing, nothing at all!"

She put down her head and cried so hard that General Washington stopped dancing and came over to her.

"Colonel Page," he said sternly, "what have you done to this young lady?"

Polly looked up and smiled through her tears.

"Nothing, sir," she said. "I was just being a silly girl and crying for fear he might be hurt—or—killed in battle. I wish you'd dance with me again, sir. That would make me feel ever so much better . . ."

General Washington smiled.

"Your permission, Colonel?" he said.

"Of course, sir," Ethan grinned. He felt vastly relieved.

He rode with Polly one night at the end of that summer of disenchantment, during which the war came to a stop and the men deserted in droves from boredom, from inactivity, and from fear of the terrible discipline by which General Washington tried to whip them into soldiers. You couldn't make a soldier of a man by making him straddle a sharp board six feet off the ground with weights tied to his feet. That only made him faint, and sometimes maimed him. And twenty-one to three hundred lashes on the bare back, washed down with brine afterwards, didn't help a man's morale either, especially when he often died of the treatment. . . .

He didn't talk to Polly at first. He just looked at her and was troubled. She was troubled, too. Her uncle Peter was threatening to send her back to New York if she didn't stop her unmaidenly behavior. After all, young ladies weren't supposed to disappear from their guardians' homes and be gone for hours without explanation. He'd even heard that she'd been consorting with the rebels . . .

"I," Polly told him, "have been seeing the man I love and mean to marry. As for consorting with the rebels, I am a rebel. I hope the colonials drive these lobster-backs into the sea!"

Then she had walked out of the house before Peter Knowles recovered from his speechlessness.

But she didn't tell Ethan that. She rode along very quietly beside him, looking at him with so much love, and longing, and hopelessness that Ethan couldn't bear to see her face in the moonlight.

He drew up his horse.

"Polly," he said, "I—I'm going away—tomorrow. We march upon Canada, Polly . . ."

Polly didn't answer him. She climbed down slowly from her mount. She walked over and sat down on the roots of a big tree.

"Come here, Ethan," she said.

Ethan got down, and went over to her. Very simply, she put up her arms to him.

Gently Ethan's hands closed over her wrists, and drew her arms down and away from him.

"No, Polly," he said quietly, "we cannot begin a thing that neither of us can finish. I could marry you, knowing how easily I could come to love you after-wards. But I don't think you'd like that. I don't want you wondering if I think sometimes of Kathy. Wait, Polly, until I am entirely free of her—and I shall be free of her, I think. Wait until I am free of danger—and of death . . . Then, I can ask you; but not until then. . . ."

She straightened up and sat there looking at him.

She didn't say anything or even cry. She just looked at him. Then, very slowly, she stood up.

"Help me to mount," she said.

Ethan helped her up, then swung into his own saddle. His mind was made up now. Polly or not, he had to join that march to Canada. He had to.

When Polly got back to Peter Knowles' house, she found her mother in tears, and her uncle Peter in a towering rage.

"I will not countenance such impudence!" he roared. "Look, Gertrude, 'tis past ten o'clock, and she has not a word for where she has been and what she has been doing. I tell you . . ."

"I'm sorry, Uncle Peter," Polly said gently, "for my rudeness this afternoon. 'Twas wicked of me. But where I was and what I was doing were not wickedness. I have been out on the Cambridge Road, past the American camp. I spent the time very sweetly, with the man I love. I know it doesn't look right, Mamma, and Uncle Peter, but nothing is right now. He has fought, he has to go on fighting—with almost nothing, no food, no ammunition, untrained men. Maybe he will have to die. Mama, you know what love is, even if Uncle Peter doesn't. Would you deny me this? I ride with him, and talk—he—he doesn't even kiss me, though I'm dying for him to . . ."

Peter Knowles was on the border of apoplexy. He threw up his hands in a gesture of utter bafflement.

"I think you see now, Gertrude," he growled, "that this matter is beyond me. So unmaidenly a young female should be in her own father's care."

Polly smiled at him.

"I'll go pack my things," she said.

So it was that when Ethan Page got back to Cambridge the last of February 1776, he found her gone. He had gone through hell that winter. He had marched almost to Quebec with Dan Morgan and Benedict Arnold and Aaron Burr. He was alive now because his own men had refused to desert him when he had fallen in the snow from exhaustion and starvation after having given them his own meager share of the food.

His boys had deserted then, bearing his unconscious form back to Fort Ticonderoga, and there Ethan had spent December and January and February with Allen and Knox, returning to Cambridge at last with Henry Knox, bringing the fifty-five field pieces on forty-two sledges that Ethan Allen was sending to George Washington to use against Boston. . . .

Ethan waited in Cambridge for Polly to ride out into the camp. She had no way of knowing he was back, he knew; but surely she'd come out to obtain some news of him.

But she didn't. And Ethan worried. He got a message into the city by one of the peddlers who passed freely between both camps. He couldn't be sure that she even got the message.

Finally he discovered from a Tory whom he'd captured on the Cambridge Road that Polly had been sent back to New York on one of her uncle's coastal sloops. The overland journey was now too dangerous.

My just desserts, he told himself wryly; how could I expect her to wait for me when I couldn't even bring myself to tell her I loved her the night we said good-by?

From Charlestown, Dorchester Heights, Lechmere's Point, and Roxbury, the cannon General Knox and

Colonel Page had brought down from Ticonderoga frowned down upon Boston. Getting those guns was luck, fortune favoring the brave. Out at sea, that same month, an American privateer captured the British supply ship *Nancy*. Among the stores taken were two thousand round shot, and a hundred thousand flints. Fate, the hand of God, had done for Washington again what the bumbling, incompetent Congress could never bring itself around to do.

On March fourth, 1776, General Washington loosed across the Charles from Roxbury the most terrible bombardment the British had ever heard. At the noise of guns, at the news of General Thomas' march toward Dorchester Heights, the men who had deserted in the autumn flocked back again. They came marching into camp, roaring drunk, bringing their own guns with them, their own food supplies, singing songs that nobody has ever put down on paper because their words would have scorched the pages.

So it was that when Howe woke up that morning of March fifth, he rubbed his eyes and gazed at a huge breastworks of hay and dirt and blocks of ice. Thomas' men had put it up overnight. Now they lay behind it, waiting for Howe to attack.

But Howe wasn't going to attack. His stomach still turned over every time he thought of Breed's Hill. He held conferences with his staff. His troops stood by, half dead on their feet from cold and disease, and waited with numbed horror for Lord Howe to order them up that hill to die.

But Lord Howe was a kindly man. Before the war, he had been a Whig, and had made speeches in favor of the American colonists. Maybe he didn't even want to beat them. And there was the lovely blond Mrs. Loring, indirectly one of the greatest heroines of the Revolution because of the fact that by keeping his lordship's attention fixed upon gentler matters, she saved thousands of American lives.

Howe's troops were sick. An epidemic of smallpox had carried off hundreds of them. And the British Parliament wasn't much better than the American Congress when it came to supplies. The redcoats dined off frozen salt beef, hard as wood, lean as carrion, and rusty as the devil. They drank raw rum and spruce liquor, which cut their insides to pieces and had them trotting all day long to the latrines by the hundreds. They died from the food and the cold, from smallpox and pneumonia.

The officers had it better. But they had too warm beds, too good liquor, and too many parties.

It was Cecil Fitzgerald who told the Knowles household what was going to happen. When Kathy heard what the plan was, she shook her golden head and stamped her pretty foot.

"Sail to Halifax?" she said. "Not me! I'm sorry, Cecil, but it's cold enough here . . ."

"But Kathy, love," Cecil pointed out, "we can't leave you here at the mercy of the rebels. Your uncle's a known King's man. They might subject you to all kinds of indignities."

"We'll go back to New York," Kathy said firmly. "Polly wrote me by one of my uncle's captains that the rebels have ceased to bother the loyalists there. They're too busy trying to find some means to save their own hides when our fleet gets there. Besides, Cecil, I'd rather take a chance on the rebels any day than freeze to death in Nova Scotia."

"But Kathy," Cecil whispered, "that means it'll be ever so long before I see you again . . ."

"Not too long, darling," Kathy murmured. "Why, you'll take New York from the rebels as easy as . . ."

"As easy as they're taking Boston from us," Cecil said bitterly.

On March seventeenth, the British evacuated Boston. Cecil had been sure that because of his rank and his position he would have been able to find a place for his beloved Kathy on the transport. He had had no idea of taking her family along. It was in the back part of his mind that by convincing Peter Knowles he was saving his niece from an unnamable fate, the doddering old fool would let him take Kathy away. And once away from the protection of her uncle . . .

But Kathy had spoiled all that. All the handsome young lordling could do now was to swear in baffled rage and hope the girls of Nova Scotia were a little less difficult.

But neither he nor his august commander were prepared for what actually happened. Hundreds of the richest, and most distinguished, citizens of the Massachusetts Colony, came to the wharf with their families and their belongings. They knelt down in the mud and half-melted snow and begged to be taken aboard with tears in their eyes.

They were good men and true. They had been loyal to their King, their town, their colony. And now a horde of tattered riffraff were going to sweep down over them. Drunken, twanging countrymen, blackguards and thieves. All the horrors that had been heaped upon the heads of loyalists in the other colonies were going to be visited upon them here.

Lord Howe was nothing if not a kindly man. He sighed, but he managed to herd them all into the dark holes of his ships, smelling to high heaven of disease and filth. They were a pitiful lot. They were good people, the pillars of society, the good steady conservatives without whom any nation soon falls to pieces, upon whom even the fiery architects of any new order soon are forced to depend. The men with the brains, the character, and the know-how.

But now they had to sail away to bleak exile in a gale-lashed land beside a frozen sea.

From the stern of the sloop *Trudy*, Peter Knowles, his sister-in-law Gertrude, the tragic Lawrences, and Kathy watched the white spread of canvas of the British fleet beating northward. The *Trudy* boiled southward under a freshing wind, from almost dead astern, heeled over hard, the white water foaming behind her. A New England-built sloop is a fast sailer. They soon dropped the King's fleet out of sight over the horizon.

"Poor Cecil," Kathy sighed, but even as she did, she couldn't help wondering which one would get to New York first, Cecil or Ethan.

Fair April was on the land when Ethan Page arrived in New York with General Washington's troops, and the British were nowhere in sight. All the trees were in blossom, and the air was soft and slumberous with spring. He hadn't much to do, for nobody, except General Nat Greene, knew what to do. Greene made the only sensible suggestion:

"Burn the blamed place to the ground and clear out!" he growled.

Washington recoiled in horror from that idea. He never could break himself of his civilian-trained delusion that towns were worth anything. But then even the trained British Generals had the same tomfool idea. The only good reason for taking a town is to smash up powder plants and cannon foundries, and New York had neither. Nor could it supply food and drink. It had to be supplied itself. And to the possessor of a fine fleet, Manhattan Island was the best target in the world —especially since Washington's shore batteries had nothing like the weight of ball and range of the guns on Lord Richard Howe's men-of-war. The brothers Howe were going to have themselves a picnic.

So Washington puttered around, fortifying Brooklyn Heights in order to close the East River. His guns on the shore of the Hudson were to prevent the British fleet from sailing up that river. Very fine. The only trouble with that was that if the British kept close to the Jersey shore, his balls couldn't even reach them.

But Ethan was home. His own personal strategy for assaulting the hearts of the Misses Knowles—because by now it was a matter of a tossed coin with Ethan— was as bad as General Washington's military tactics. He sought out his father and obtained a sum of gold from him. With it, he commissioned a tailor to make him one of the finest uniforms the Continental Army was ever to see in its barebacked history.

It was the worst error he ever made. And his luck was as bad as his tactics. When he dismounted in front of the Knowles' home on William Street, Kathy was sitting on the stoop. Polly was in the house, helping her mother and the maid with the laundry. Kathy was as lazy as a lovely kitten. She avoided work with effortless ease.

She stood up when he came through the gate, her violet eyes widening.

"Ethan!" she breathed. "How fine you are!"

Kathy loved uniforms. And somehow Cecil's scarlet coat seemed very far away then. Kathy was lonely—Ethan was here. Cecil was not.

He stood there frowning at her. He opened his mouth to say, "Where's Polly?" but he never got it out. It was April and the sun was soft and warm. Some of the light tangled in Kathy's golden hair and blazed. He just stood there, staring at her.

"Ethan," Kathy purred, "aren't you going to kiss me?"

"Should think," Ethan growled, "you've been kissed enough by the lobsterbacks."

Kathy smiled at him.

"You're jealous," she murmured, and took hold of his crossed shoulder straps. "You shouldn't be jealous, Ethan. You know I really *do* love you . . ."

Then going up on tiptoe, she kissed him expertly and well, employing all the tricks she had learned from that professional lady-killer, Cecil Fitzgerald, of His Majesty's Royal Grenadier Guards.

Ethan stood there very stiffly for a long moment. But he had been in love with Kathy Knowles all his life. And Kathy was beautiful. Ethan was neither wood nor stone. He knew positively which of the two girls was the better. The finer, sweeter, more loyal. But that was sense. And a man's head and his heart are seldom on speaking terms.

His arms swept around her waist and drew her to

him. And then his luck ran out. All the way out. For ten seconds before Gertrude Knowles had sent Polly to call her sister to help them hang up the wash.

Polly stood there looking at them. It was a long time before either of them noticed her presence.

"Polly!" Ethan gasped.

"Hello, Ethan," Polly said. Her voice was very low, but her control was superb. "You'll excuse Kathy, won't you? Mother needs her. She can come back in a few minutes . . ."

Then she turned and went back into the house. Against the misery of his gaze, her back was very stiff and proud.

CHAPTER 6

Polly brought the glass of brandy into her father's study. Patrick took it from her, clutching it with both hands. That was the only way he could hold a glass now. If he tried to hold it with one hand alone, it shook so that the brandy spilled all over his waistcoat.

Polly stood there looking at him. He was dirty, unshaven. There were brandy and food stains on his waistcoat. He didn't look at her any more. He seemed to have difficulty raising his eyes to gaze into anybody's face.

What happened to him while we were away? What dreadful thing? Polly thought.

Even using both hands he couldn't steady the brandy glass. Red trickles of brandy spilled down from both corners of his mouth. His long clay pipe lay on the floor where he had dropped it. It was broken.

Polly bent and picked it up.

"Papa," she said, "why are you like this? What happened to you? Tell me, what?"

Patrick Knowles looked rapidly around the study. He seemed to be searching for watchers in the shadow.

"Jason Goodby!" he whispered. "The—Sons of Liberty—they—they——"

"What did they do, Papa?"

"They—they——"

"Yes, Papa?"

"They took me—away—to a—a farm, I think. Then they——" He looked at his daughter as though she were a stranger. "I don't know what they did," he said hoarsely. "I can't remember . . ."

Polly left the study. She stopped in the hall to blink back her tears. She had gotten this far with her father before. But she knew now she'd never get the truth from him. The Patrick Knowles she had known was gone, and in his place was this shattered wreck who didn't even look like him any more. This pitiful, beaten stranger . . .

She heard Kathy chattering with Ethan in the sitting room. That was another thing. Patrick had shown Ethan the door, branding him a traitor. But now Ethan was welcome again. For when Gertrude had asked him about it—at Kathy's request—he had sunk down into his chair and quavered:

"Let him come. 'Tis better not to anger them, Gert —at least not until Lord Howe's fleet appears. . . ."

Polly fled upstairs to her room. She certainly didn't intend to stand there and listen to Ethan and Kathy. Nor, by all that was holy, was she going to sit upstairs and mope. For if Lieutenant William Pikes wasn't Ethan Page, he was still a very presentable young man and very pleasant company.

So it was that Ethan Page and Kathy happened to meet another couple in the path that moonlit night. It was not until the young Lieutenant saluted that he recognized him. It was Will Pikes, one of his own aides. And the girl with Will was Polly Knowles.

Ethan stood quite still. There was something moving in his chest just below his heart. He was having the strangest difficulty with his breathing.

" 'Lo, Ethan," Polly said.

Ethan bowed. It wasn't a good bow. It was a little stiff. The motion was jerky.

"A pleasant evening to you, Polly," he said. "And to you, Lieutenant."

"Thank you, sir," Will said shyly.

Kathy stared at Ethan. There was a strangeness in his voice. She didn't like the sound of it. She tried to read his face. With nothing but moonlight, that was hard to do.

She looked at Polly. Polly's dark eyes were like the night—filled with shadows. And Katherine Knowles remembered all those hours when Polly had ridden off alone in Boston. . . .

They moved on finally, after the situation had been weighted down with silence that crawled along four sets of nerves. Kathy didn't say anything but her mind was busy.

What's happened between them? she thought. Polly looked at him then like—like she owns him. I wonder if there's more between them than I thought?

The idea rankled. Kathy loved to make men jealous. But now she was having her first real experience with that feeling. And it was real. Before the war, it had never occurred to her that anything would ever come between her and Ethan. She had been quite content with the idea of marrying him. That she was unable to love anyone with the depth and sincerity and single-mindedness that Polly was capable of was her misfortune. But she was fond of Ethan in a sort of light and laughing way. The only person she cared about with any real emotion was herself. She would have been just as jealous had a similar thing happened involving Cecil

Fitzgerald. She was capable of being jealous of anyone who disturbed the position of any of the males who hovered about her, their adoring faces reflecting her beauty and her charm like so many mirrors. If they were turned away so that she couldn't see that reflection, her vanity suffered. And Kathy's vanity was her life.

And Patrick Knowles' older daughter was far from stupid. She had a very good and practical mind. The only trouble with it was that it saw everything in the light of the ultimate effect it might have upon the life and happiness of Kathy Knowles. She was incapable of any loyalties except to herself.

She knew, without even having to think about it very hard, that it was a good idea to have more than one string to your fiddle. Of course, the British were going to win. How could this tattered rabble stand against them? And once they had won, it would be very fine to sail to London in style, live in a castle, and have hundreds of flunkies to bow to every whim of her ladyship, the new Lady Fitzgerald, Viscountess Linkletter.

But the British hadn't won yet. And this tattered rabble had beaten the tar out of them nearly every time they had met. If by some miracle the Colonials did win, it would be almost as fine to be married to this tall, handsome man sure to rise to eminence in the councils of the Republic. Secretary of State Page of the United States of America and lovely wife, Mistress Kathy Page, today entertained the ambassador of . . .

Ethan's face was so still.

"Ethan," she said, drawing close to him, "I've changed my mind. Let's go to that banquet after all . . ."

"As you will, my love," Ethan said dryly.

The banquet was given by the New York Provincial

Assembly. It was very gay. General Washington put two bottles of Madeira under his sword belt without blinking an eye. Afterwards he showed not the slightest sign of intoxication. But when Israel Putnam tried to do the same thing, they had to carry him away from the table before the banquet was over.

"What a pity!" young Captain Gibbs said. "He's the only one here who knows all the verses to the Mollie Lauder song. . . ."

After the banquet, Kathy danced with General Washington and all the other officers who could still stand up. Except Ethan. He said he didn't feel like dancing. He sat there and didn't touch his food. But the amount of Madeira he put away was a marvel.

Kathy kept watching him out of the corner of her eye as she danced. She didn't even flirt very much. The way that Ethan looked bothered her. Finally she excused herself from her partner, General Nathanael Greene, and went over and sat down beside him.

She tried to talk to Ethan, but he was morose. So she took a sip of Madeira. It tasted good. Besides, it made her feel extraordinarily wise and capable. So she took another. And another.

Half an hour later, she and Ethan were laughing together over jokes that were utterly pointless, made no sense, and were often not even completed. At exactly the same moment, they stood up, and left the banquet hall together, still laughing. . . .

Polly sat by her window. It was past midnight. She had on her nightdress, but she hadn't been to bed. She had been sitting like that ever since Will Pikes brought her home. At first, she had had the idea of waiting up for

Kathy. She wanted to talk to her sister, to find out . . .

Just what she was going to say, Polly didn't know. And Kathy took so long to come . . . She heard the grandfather clock in the hall strike the half hour.

Then she heard the footsteps on the walk.

"Kathy," Ethan said. His voice was choked, hoarse.

"Dearest," Kathy whispered. "Oh my dearest . . ."

Polly didn't hear any more. She had already flown from the window, hurled herself on the bed, pulled a pillow over her head, and was busily pounding the mattress with both her small fists.

It was fortunate the feather mattress was so soft and that Patrick Knowles was such a sound sleeper. Else he might have awakened and met Kathy as she stole into the house, like many a willful daughter before and since, with her dancing slippers clutched in her hands.

On July tenth, George Washington called his troops together and had the Declaration of Independence read to them. Ethan thought it was an extraordinarily moving document. It was filled with big, fine, fighting words. He wanted to rush off and tell Kathy about it. Then it came to him that Kathy wouldn't understand it, or would have scant enthusiasm for it, if she did.

His footsteps slowed. He was one of the most troubled young men in the entire Army. He couldn't understand what was happening to him. He had asked Kathy to marry him. He had asked her many times. But her answer was always the same:

"No, dearest, not yet. But let's wait until this horrible war is over. It'll be so much nicer then . . ."

He had the feeling she was waiting, calculating her chances, seeing which way the victory winds would blow. It wasn't a good feeling. It took the fine edge off all his rapture. What was worse, he couldn't go to the Knowles' house without occasionally meeting Polly and seeing the death in her eyes.

Today, he didn't go there at all. He went off to a tavern and toasted Tom Jefferson's masterpiece alone.

Two days later, the lower bay was white with the sails of the British fleet. The redcoats landed on Staten Island, and everybody waited. Kathy Knowles became visibly less affectionate at the thought of Cecil Fitzgerald waiting with that fleet. And Ethan Page cursed himself for seven different kinds of a fool and drank a pint of brandy every night to stun himself into sleep.

The waiting was broken, finally; but not by the redcoats. Polly Knowles woke up to the sound of hoofbeats in William Street, early in the morning. She was at the door before Ethan reached it.

"Trouble, Polly," he said. "The Tories tried to murder General Washington. Paris green in his peas at dinner last night—put there by Tom Hickey, his own bodyguard. They're hanging Hickey this morning, and the mobs are on the loose. Go get dressed. Get your mother and father up—and Kathy. Tell them to stay away from the windows. And keep calm, won't you?"

Polly flew up the stairs. By limiting herself to one petticoat, she managed to get dressed in less than ten minutes. She didn't awaken the others. There was time enough for that later. No point in having to quell hysteria now before it was really necessary.

Instead she went into her father's study and took down a small beautiful fowling piece. She loaded it expertly. She had often done that for her father on duck shoots as a child. She slung a powder horn over one shoulder and picked up a bag of bird shot. Then she went back to her window and waited.

She didn't have long to wait. She heard their drunken howls long before they reached the house.

Ethan sat on the stoop, and smoked his pipe. He didn't move. The mob came roaring up to the gate. When they saw him there, splendid in his buff and blue regimentals, they stopped.

Ethan took the pipe out of his mouth.

"All right, you blackguards," he said quietly. "Off with you."

The leader of the mob was riding a horse. He was dressed in rags, but the horse was very fine, so Polly knew he must have stolen it. He had a rusty saber in his hand. He had a hard time staying in the saddle.

"Who might you be?" he growled at Ethan.

"Colonel Page of the Continental Army," Ethan said. "And you, my unwashed friend?"

"That don't matter. What be you a-doing there on the stoop of King's men?"

"Resting," Ethan smiled. "Thought I might have a little pistol practice while I rested, though. And the first man who steps through that gate is going to be the target. Do I make myself clear?"

Polly could see the fear in their faces. But there was something else, too. Rage. Drunken craft.

Carelessly, Ethan lifted the pistols.

"Harkee, Nat," one of the rioters called, "there be but one o' him and fifty o' us. Let's rush him!"

"Wa-al now," the leader began, and swayed so far that he had to catch the pommel of his saddle to keep from falling off.

Then Polly did precisely the right thing. She lifted the fowling piece and let the horse have a charge of buckshot in the flank. The animal reared, screaming. Nat went over backwards out of the saddle. The horse continued to rear so that the mob had to scatter like so many ants to get from under those ironshod hoofs.

Ethan lifted his pistols and fired two shots over their heads. They ran. Like rats. Nat scrambled up out of the dust, and pounded behind them, yelling:

"Wait for me, boys! F'God's sake wait for me!"

"Come on down, Polly," Ethan called. "Sure you don't want a commission in the Army?"

Polly came down the stairs and stood beside him, smiling. But the smile didn't last very long. For Kathy came flying out of the door and threw her arms about Ethan.

"Oh, Ethan!" she cried. "I saw them! Those horrible, horrible creatures! And you saved us, my darling—you saved us all . . ."

"No," Ethan grinned, "matter of fact, I didn't. Polly shot the horse out from under the leader, and they took to their heels." He stood there looking at Polly.

"Your little sister," he said to Kathy, "is a very brave girl."

But I'm not, Polly wailed inside her heart, on that morning of August twenty-seventh, hearing the guns. Ethan thinks I'm brave, but I'm not brave enough for this! Why do they have to fight their battles in sight and sound of our cities?

She went up on the roof, but the Heights of Brooklyn were too far away. All she could see was the gun smoke rising under the cloudy sky; all she could hear was the leaden booming of the guns.

She looked southward toward the bay. The masts of Lord Howe's fleet were still there. Thank God for that, she thought, because she knew what Ethan feared. All Howe needed to do was to send a few men-of-war up the East River, and the forces that George Washington had sent to Brooklyn would be caught between William Howe's army and Richard Howe's fleet and crushed like rats in a trap. Now Ethan and the others had a chance. A slight chance; but still a chance. . . .

She would have been sick with fear had she known how slight that chance was.

Ethan knew, and resigned himself to death. He had known since yesterday, when he saw George Washington, in a thunderous burst of profanity, dismiss four hundred Connecticut Mounted Rangers from the field because they wouldn't dismount and serve as infantry.

"Great balls of fire!" Ethan exploded. "Doesn't he know what cavalry is for?"

"You're out of order, Colonel," General Nat Greene said sternly. Then he dropped his voice to a whisper: "God save us from all the things he doesn't know!"

Ethan spent the whole night of August twenty-sixth thinking of his own follies and mistakes. Among the things he blamed himself for was loving Kathy, whom he shouldn't instead of Polly, whom he should. But by morning, he was resigned. After all, he couldn't change things now. He and the others were going to die because their Commander in Chief had decided to hold an untenable position like New York City, which was valueless from the military standpoint, had split forces inferior in numbers to the enemy in two, thus doubling their inferiority, had placed both his feeble forces upon islands in sight of a foe whose fleet commanded the sea, and had dismissed the very cavalry which was his only means of finding out where Sir William's troops were, which way they were going to march, and the extent of their numbers. . . .

There may have been worse Generals in the history of warfare than George Washington, but at the moment, Ethan doubted it profoundly.

At dusk of the twenty-ninth, Ethan stood on the bank of the East River, supervising the loading of the pitiful remnants of the American Army into rowboats. He was stunned beyond tears by what had happened to his men. They had been ordered to fight in the open, in parade-ground formations, against the finest army in the world. They had been slaughtered.

He looked at the fog rolling in the sea. God was still with them—the God Who had sent the rain which sent the British scurrying for their tents instead of finishing the massacre, Who had kept up the drizzle all day yesterday and today, and Who had blessed General Howe with such a powerful sense of the fitness of things that he refused to fight in the rain, and Lord Richard Howe with such a divine density of wit that he had never thought of sending the fleet up the river to cut them off.

Yes, God was with them. That very special God Who takes care of fools and children.

Ethan stayed with his men until the last of them was off in the half-rotten, leaky rowboats. He died a thousand deaths that night, because the fog was luminous with moonlight. He kept straining his ears for the thud of Hessian boots, or the crackle of musketry. But Sir William didn't come.

He was almost the last man off Fulton Ferry. There was only one boat behind him. In it George Washington sat, sick at heart at all the slaughter his own folly had caused. In the east, dawn was graying the sky. And when that last boat was a hundred yards offshore, the British regulars came pounding up on the double.

It was bad melodrama, farce. It was something out of a play that gentleman Johnny Burgoyne might have written. For all those British regulars stood there shooting from the waist, and not a shot came near General Washington.

Colonel Ethan Page permitted himself one moment of bitterness. He had seen his own troops cut to pieces, bayoneted, murdered.

It's a pity, he thought, they're such bad shots. If they got him, we might get ourselves a real General—somebody like Greene or Arnold. . . .

"You," Kathy Knowles said to Ethan, stifling a yawn, "make me awfully tired, sometimes . . ."

Ethan looked at her. He felt sick. There was a tight little ball of rage and disgust down at the pit of his stomach.

"Playing both ends against the middle, Kathy?" he said. "Waiting like a cat to see who'll win so you'll know which way to jump?"

Kathy smiled a little.

"Waiting?" she said. "But Ethan, I don't have to wait. Not for that. You know yourself who's going to win. I heard you tell Polly yesterday that Nat Greene

and Charles Lee want to burn the city and clear out.
If it weren't for the fact that your Commander in Chief
is such a monumental idiot, you'd be gone by now . . ."

"And if I were?" Ethan said grimly.

"I'd be sorry, of course," Kathy said, "but———"

"But not sorry enough to prevent you from changing
sides again. Not enough to stay away from British
officers—even perhaps to forget I ever existed and
marry one of them."

"Now really, Ethan . . ."

"I'm right, and you know it."

Kathy turned upon him.

"What do you expect of me, Ethan? I'm young. On
what basis should I resign myself to becoming a widow
—and of a man who's going to be hanged at that? Tell
me, Ethan—what?"

Ethan looked at her. His face was very still.

"On the basis of love and loyalty," he said quietly.
"But you don't understand those words, do you,
Kathy? Neither of them . . ."

"I understand you're very tiresome, Ethan," Kathy
said. "Very tiresome—and a fool."

Then she turned and went back into the house.
Ethan stood there a long time after she had gone. Then
he mounted and rode off slowly down the street.

On September fifteenth, 1776, Ethan was with General
Washington and the rest of his aides in a cornfield on
East Forty-second Street trying to stop the rout of the
American Army. The men were throwing away their
muskets, knapsacks, powder pouches, and running like
sheep. Washington was everywhere at once, slashing at
them with his whip, swearing until the air blistered blue

about his head and the very wind had the smell of brimstone in it. But he couldn't stop them. They fled west along that path until they crossed Fifth Avenue.

Washington and his aides stopped them there, but only for a moment. Not even the flat of Ethan's sword could stop his men from running. Washington's horse-whip drew blood, but they didn't even feel it. They whirled on past, ghost-white, trembling. Ethan and the others rode after them. There was nothing else to do.

But at the last moment, Ethan looked back. He saw General Washington sitting there in the saddle, facing the British vanguard, unmoving and alone.

Ethan felt a tight knot at the base of his throat, shutting off his breath. He had been bitter at his Commander. He had blamed him for the death of men become comrades, friends. But now, seeing him sitting there, gaunt and bowed on his big white horse, all the bitterness drained out of Ethan Page. He felt a great surge of love for this man who couldn't run. This man who preferred death to disgrace. This beaten man trying now to die with honor. The bullets whined about him, but he sat there like a rock upon his white stallion facing the enemy. And Ethan knew he must not let his Commander die.

He whirled his own black horse and spurred back to General Washington. Something of that magic talisman that rode forever with George Washington into battle shed its influence around Ethan Page. The air was alive with the whistle of grape and ball, but nothing touched him. He reached the Commander's side.

"General," he got out, "you can't stay here!"

Washington looked at him. The gray eyes probed through him, beyond him, fixed upon death and disaster.

Ethan snatched the bridle from his General's hand, and led him from that field by force. And George Washington, slumped in the saddle, stared at the earth, and let himself be led.

Five days later, at dawn, Ethan stood outside his tent on Harlem Heights and stared at the red glow in the sky. It grew brighter. Smoke plumed above it. Sparks flew through the smoke.

"By thunder!" a soldier at his side cried. "They're burning New York!"

He was wrong. The British dearly loved towns. They had no intention of burning the city and thus forcing themselves to spend the winter in huts and tents. They said American spies set the blaze. But Washington had faced destruction rather than burn New York. The redcoats caught some of the Sons of Liberty and hanged them over the burning ruins to roast. They bound a few more patriots, and threw them into the flames. More than a thousand houses in the district around and below Wall Street sank to the ground in ashes. And nobody ever found out who started it.

But Ethan Page could only stand there and watch that glow brighten and curse the fate that prevented him from spurring to Kathy's aid. *I'm a fool to even want to help her,* he thought, *but I do. God help me, I do!*

Kathy stood that very moment a little apart from her family and watched the blaze. Polly and her mother were holding Patrick Knowles by both his arms. Gertrude and Patrick were both crying, but Patrick was behaving much worse than his wife.

"Gone!" he groaned. "All gone! Everything I've worked for! Let me go, Gertie! Let me go back and die and be done with it! We're ruined, I tell you, ruined!"

"Hush, Papa," Polly said.

Kathy didn't say anything. She didn't even cry. She just stood there and wondered what it was that kept the barn from catching afire while the house blazed to high heaven.

She was standing there like that when Major Cecil Fitzgerald, of His Majesty's Grenadier Guards, galloped into the street.

"Sorry, Kathy," he said, "deuced sorry. Rotten show, what?"

Kathy looked at him. Then with perfectly calculated timing, she burst into tears.

"Oh, Cecil!" she wailed. "What are we going to do?"

Cecil took her into his arms.

"Don't worry, Katherine," he murmured, "I'll arrange everything."

He rode away, telling them to wait where they were. Two hours later he was back, a smile on his much too handsome face. Behind him came a landau with a British private driving.

"Get in, please," Cecil said, "all of you." When they were seated he turned to Patrick Knowles with beguiling earnestness.

"Very sorry, sir," he said, "but I've had difficulties. You know how crowded New York is. I've found quarters for you all, but they are, unfortunately, widely separated. The Tiltons, whom you know well, sir, have consented to take you and Mistress Knowles in. Dr. Rawls and his wife can provide a cot in a hallway for Polly. As for Kathy, there is space at the Widow

Horton's, but she'll have to share occupancy—with another tenant—which is why I couldn't lodge your daughters together, sir, as I know you would have preferred . . ."

Patrick nodded without speaking. He was beyond caring.

But Polly studied Cecil's face. There was something familiar about that name Horton. The widow Horton's. She searched her memory, but nothing came. She turned toward Kathy.

Kathy was staring at Cecil with her violet eyes opened wide. She sat up very stiffly in the landau. Then, very slowly, she relaxed. A smile lighted her eyes.

The Widow Horton's, Polly thought. Now where the dickens have I heard that name?

She didn't find out though, not then. For Cecil so arranged matters that her parents were conducted to their new lodgings first. Then he took her to Dr. Rawls' and drove off with Kathy, alone.

"Cecil," Kathy whispered, when they were alone in the landau, with another soldier riding Cecil's horse behind them, "I know the Widow Horton's. She has that big house on Thirty-second Street, and she lets rooms to—to British officers, Cecil . . ."

"You're quite right," Cecil said.

"Cecil—who is this other tenant I'm to share with?"

Cecil smiled at her.

"Can't you guess?" he said.

Kathy stared at him, sitting bolt upright in the little carriage. The sunlight came through the smoke of the burning houses, and touched his spotless bagwig. His coat glowed scarlet, and his pale, handsome face was alight with joy, and mischief, and desire.

Kathy was vain, and fickle, and thoughtless; but she was a Knowles. And there never was a Knowles in all human history who was ever completely a fool.

"Very well," she said. "But know one thing, my scheming Cecil: my first request to the Widow Horton shall be for my own room with a stout iron lock, and a big key, which I shall have placed on the inside of my door. 'Tis true I love you, but not like that. If you can't offer me an honorable love—then I'll have none at all, thank you!"

Cecil Fitzgerald frowned, briefly. But he was young, and overwhelmingly confident of his skill in such matters. He straightened up, smiling.

"To Mistress Horton's," he said to the driver.

The trouble was, he had never known Patrick Knowles. And Kathy was Patrick's daughter—after all. . . .

CHAPTER 7

"Glorious news, Gertrude!" Peter Knowles said. "Knyphausen and his Hessians have taken Fort Washington. 'Tis said that the rebels' Commander in Chief is among the prisoners. The rebellion is all but over . . . Where's Patrick? This news will be some comfort to him, or I miss my guess . . ."

"Sleeping," Gertrude whispered. "Please, Piet, do not disturb him. With him it grows worse all the time—the weakness, and the weeping . . ."

"Poor devil," Peter Knowles said with feeling. "I shall be glad to see the authors of his misfortunes hanged!"

Polly got up and walked over to her uncle. She was glad he had come down to New York to help them out. He'd found them a house, buying it outright from a Tory family gone back to England. He managed the important business, which was as flourishing as ever, despite losses from the American privateers. Perhaps a little more so, because the British officers bought vast quantities of the Antilles rum. Uncle Peter didn't disapprove of her quite so much now. The rebels were safely on the run. They had been driven off of Harlem Heights after seven days of hell; at White Plains, the British cavalry had ridden them to earth; then the retreat into New Jersey, with young Alexander Hamilton covering them with his artillery.

And now, the last outpost of the rebels in New York had fallen. No wonder Uncle Peter thought she'd come to her senses.

"Did they take many prisoners?" she asked.

"Nearly three thousand," Peter said, "and all their munitions and supplies. They're going to march the prisoners through the streets this morning. Too bad I won't be able to see it; but business before pleasure, Polly."

He patted her affably upon the head. One of the reasons her uncle was nice to her now was that her actions reassured him after the shock that Kathy had given him, when she had chosen to stay on at the Widow Horton's and cut herself off from her family.

Half an hour later, Polly Knowles stood in the crowd that watched the beaten American prisoners being marched down the Island. The Hessians led a tall man along, apart from the others. But Polly, who knew George Washington well, saw that the Germans had made a mistake. They hadn't captured the Commander in Chief. The man they led so proudly was Colonel Maxwell, one of his aides.

She stood there, scanning the long line of dirty, ragged prisoners, a wild hope stirring in her heart. If Ethan were taken, he'd be safe. She wouldn't have to worry any more. There wouldn't be any more nightmares in which she saw him lying on the muddy earth soaked with his own blood.

If he lived, there'd be hope. Kathy was gone now. When the war was over, Ethan would come to her. She was sure of that. But he'd have to come of his own free will. Never again, Polly swore, will I make a move in his direction. He'll have to come to me, and he'll have to beg. I must be sure. I won't have him by default. 'Twill do him good to suffer a little. Heaven knows I've suffered enough on his behalf.

But when she finally saw him trudging along in that sad line, despair in his face, she wept. The tears were partly of joy. Ethan was out of it now. Those prisoner-of-war camps on Staten Island were terrible, but he'd live through that. And through Cecil, as hard as it was now to have to ask him, considering the circumstances, she would arrange it so she could see Ethan and take him food and clothing to keep him alive.

I won't be a fool about him any more, she thought. But I can't let him suffer too much. I can't let him die.

Without being conscious of it, she was walking southward, toward the tip of Manhattan. Then around the corner swirled a horde of women. Polly was quite accustomed to that kind of women now. She looked at them calmly, thinking:

What is it about war that so debases a man's taste?

Then all the women, fiercely pro-British now that the King's troops had occupied the town, marched along beside those poor bedraggled devils, screaming:

"Which one is Washington? Show us Washington! We want Washington! Let us entertain him, me Lords!"

They decided that the handsome Colonel Maxwell must be the Commander in Chief. They swarmed over him, pulling his hair, clawing at his eyes, spitting in his face.

Then one of them saw Ethan Page. His splendid uniform was rumpled and torn now, but it was still fine. And Ethan was a handsome lad.

"Here be another fine one!" the women yelled. "Lord but he be pretty! Come 'ere, me fine boy, and let me give you a buss—cheer you up right smart, if you ask me!"

Then she leaped upon Ethan, wrapping her scrawny arms about his neck.

Pin points of fire gathered in Polly's eyes, blazed. She looked around her quickly, and saw a coach sitting there filled with grinning Tories, observing this parade. There was a whip in the socket. Five seconds later, Polly had it.

The Hessian guards roared with laughter at their prisoners' efforts to defend themselves from the women of the town. A minute later, they were laughing even harder. Because Polly Knowles descended upon the woman who was tormenting Ethan with her unsavory attentions and swung that whip through a high arc and brought it whistling down.

It cut through the woman's rags like a knife, bringing blood. Polly swung it again and again. The woman turned Ethan loose and whirled, but Polly slashed her to the earth and continued to lash her, the whip whistling through the air, biting, and the woman crawling like a frenzied crab upon the earth, trying to get out of there. It is quite possible that Polly would have beaten her to death if a burly Hessian had not twisted the whip from Polly's hand, laughing:

"*Ach, du kleine, süsse Teufelein!* [You small, sweet devil! That's enough!] *Das ist jetz genug und mehr!*"

The whole line halted. The women stared at Polly, rage in their sweaty faces. They seemed to be gathering for a rush, but the grinning Hessians pointed their muskets at them and roared:

"*'Raus mit dich! 'Raus!*"

The women didn't understand the words, but they

could comprehend bayonets. More than once they had felt a jab or two when these Hessian lads were in a merry mood. They turned and ran off down a side street, screaming curses as they went.

"Thanks, Polly," Ethan said.

"Don't be flattered," Polly snapped. "I'd have done as much for any other man in the line."

"Only you didn't," Ethan grinned. "And there were others being similarly entertained . . ."

Polly stamped her foot.

"I wish I had my whip back again," she said.

But two days later she came over to Staten Island on a pass, with food for him and wine. She sat beside him as he ate. Ethan stared at her, but she avoided his eyes.

"Polly," he said, "why are you doing this?"

"I don't desert my friends," Polly said.

"And you consider me a friend of yours?"

"Yes. It wasn't your fault that I was a fool. You never tried to delude me about how you felt. Why should I hate you?"

"I'm glad you don't," Ethan said. "Tell me, Polly, if I come out of this alive—will you ever think of me as you did—again?"

Polly looked at him. Then, very slowly, she shook her head.

"No, Ethan," she said. "I've been hurt enough. I wouldn't marry you now if you were the last man alive."

She stood up, straightened her skirt.

" 'Bye, Ethan," she said. "I'll come again."

"Thank you," Ethan said. "Please do."

But Uncle Peter Knowles was wrong about one thing. The war was far from over. During those nine months between November 1776 and August 1777 that Ethan Page was a prisoner of war, that ragged, glorious rabble in arms that George Washington commanded slashed back like a pack of cornered wildcats. General Washington himself led two of the attacks, fighting and winning the battles of Trenton and Princeton with such masterful brilliance that when Ethan finally heard about them, he doubted the news. And there was General Herkimer, who murdered St. Leger's redcoats and Indians at Oriskany, while sitting under a tree, smoking a pipe and bleeding to death of his wounds. There was Benedict Arnold at Fort Stanwix, who chased St. Leger and Johnny Johnson back to Canada by sending a half-wit Dutchman named Hon Yost among the Indians with fantastic lies about the size of his forces and won a major battle without firing a shot. And that Connecticut wild man, John Stark, cut Burgoyne's detachments to bloody ribbons at Bennington.

Best of all, when Washington sent that miserable grandmother of a general, Horatio Gates, against Burgoyne at Saratoga, he was lucky enough to have one of the supreme military geniuses of all time as Gates' second-in-command. And Benedict Arnold won that battle while Gates sat in his tent and argued with a wounded British captive. But afterwards Gates took all the credit for it.

Some of these battles had a direct effect on Ethan Page's fate. They and one other thing: the fact that the British had accidentally captured Charles Lee. The battles had given Washington plenty of prisoners to exchange for his own men held captive by the British. And Charles Lee was held at Staten Island, which focused the Commander in Chief's attention on that prison. He wanted Lee back. He thought that Lee was a great General. Perhaps he vaguely associated the renegade Englishman with his friends, the Lees of Virginia; but this Lee was no kin. He wouldn't, Ethan thought bitterly, have known a great General if he saw one lit up with candles like a Christmas tree. Lee was nothing—a coward and almost a traitor—but Washington wanted him. So he exchanged prisoners for Lee and the other officers held on Staten Island. And Ethan Page got out of jail.

Polly saw him the day before he was freed. She told herself that there was nothing left between them but calm friendship—the ghost of a love now dead. That being so, why was she having such a hard time blinking back her tears?

But she knew what Ethan faced. Before him lay the smoke of battle, the long marches, the starvation, and the cold. She remembered the men she had seen lying on the earth that evening after Breed's Hill. She could picture Ethan lying like that, his face black with powder smoke, his blue eyes opened wide, staring sightlessly at a winter sky.

But it was no good to tell Ethan. A man marching out to die should go with his heart unburdened with trouble. And Polly had grown both in wisdom and in pride.

If ever we are to be together, she thought, he must come to me. Of his own free will, wanting to—not out of pity. Then what we'll have will be ours and I'll be beholden to nobody. Not even to Kathy—especially not to Kathy—a person less worthy of respect now than that woman I horse-whipped in the street!

" 'Bye, Ethan," she said. "Take care of yourself."

"I will," Ethan murmured. He searched her face. His eyes had a baffled expression in them. And something else, too—something very like pain.

Late in October, Polly Knowles had a visitor. But that was after places called Brandywine, and Paoli, and Germantown, where the trained British troops had chased the pitiful, ragged, starving farmers that Washington led from the field and holed them up at the place that they and no descendant of theirs ever were to forget. Its name was Valley Forge.

Polly had heard about those terrible defeats. She was half out of her mind from fear and worry over Ethan's fate. Her mood, when she opened her door in response to that persistent knocking, was little short of savage. When she saw who stood there, her first impulse was to slam the door in her visitor's face. But she couldn't do that to Kathy. Not to her own sister. Not even when Kathy had become the subject of common gossip and alienated herself from her family and friends. A great feeling of pity welled up within her. Whatever Kathy was doing, it was obviously taking its toll. The gay, laughing Kathy of before the war was gone. Polly noticed how wan and troubled her sister looked.

"Polly," Kathy said, "I have to ask a favor of you. . . ."

Polly didn't answer her. She just stood there, looking at her sister.

Kathy shook her head wearily.

"I know," she said, "precisely what you're thinking. But you're wrong. I'm sick of this. If I hadn't promised Cecil . . ."

"What is it that you promised Cecil?" Polly said

dryly. "To continue disgracing your good name and the reputation of our family without a thought? The only woman boarder in a house full of soldiers. Seen constantly, morning and night, with one of them—and you expect people not to talk? Or that anyone, even I, now, after one full year has gone by—not to believe them?"

"No," Kathy said quietly, "that's too much to expect, I guess—especially since I've lost your affection, Polly, over Ethan. Somehow that hurts worse than anything, Polly, to have you hate me. I never wanted it to come to that. . . ."

Polly felt something stinging behind her eyelids. She had to blink them very fast. Suddenly, impulsively, she put her two hands on Kathy's shoulders.

"Forgive me, Kathy," she said. "What do you want me to do?"

"A—a kindness," Kathy whispered. "You see, Cecil wants me to join him in Philadelphia. He's going to be down there a long time, he thinks. And I—God help me, Polly, I miss him so!"

"Then it is true!" Polly exploded. "Kathy, how could you!"

"Very easily," Kathy said. "Like any other wife—I want to be with my husband. Is that so strange?"

"Wife?" Polly gasped. "You mean you and Cecil are married?"

"And have been right from the first," Kathy said. "Dear heavens, how easy it is for people to believe the worst! I didn't mean to tell you, Polly—I promised Cecil I wouldn't tell anybody . . ."

Polly stared at her sister.

"And you let Mama cry her heart out for a year,"

she whispered, "and poor, sick Papa—Kathy, what kind of a person are you?"

"I promised Cecil," Kathy said stubbornly. "There's a lot at stake, Polly. Cecil's in line for an earldom—his father is very old, and very strict. He has a girl picked out for Cecil—a noblewoman, of course. And he's quite capable of cutting Cecil off without a penny for disobeying his wishes . . ."

"Still, I don't see . . ."

"I'm trying to explain. Cecil's father may die before the war is over. Then Cecil would automatically inherit. But if he doesn't, Cecil believes I can win the old man over. He has quite an eye for beauty, and Cecil thinks that my looks and manners may melt his icy heart. I—I don't know—it's the chance we have to take."

"So now you let everybody scorn you, and——"

"Yes—I'm strong enough, Polly. In the end I'll have my certificate of marriage, signed by the army chaplain who married us, and the witness to prove I never was what people thought. I insisted upon having proof, Polly—because I wanted most of all to make it up to Mama, and to you . . ."

"Yet Mama must go on suffering," Polly mused, "believing this . . ."

"I'm sorry, Polly; truly I am. But she'll forgive me when she knows, especially when I tell her it was to save Cecil and me from becoming penniless. . . ."

Polly looked at her sister, and her eyes were dark and sad.

"Suppose there is a child, Kathy?" she said.

"Then we'd have to end this painful pretense and risk Cecil's father learning of our marriage," Kathy said firmly.

"You still haven't told me," Polly said, "what I'm supposed to do."

"Go with me. I know so many people in Philadelphia. It would look so much better if you were there with me . . ."

"And what am I supposed to do when Cecil comes to see you? Disappear, I suppose?"

"He wouldn't come to see me. I—I'll go to him. . . ."

Polly considered the matter. It wasn't going to be easy to persuade her mother, and certainly not Uncle Peter, that she should do this for Kathy without telling them of Kathy's secret marriage. It was on the tip of her tongue to say no. But then she thought about Ethan, holed up with Washington's starving rabble at a place called Valley Forge—not far from Philadelphia— and she knew that after all she was going to have that talk with her mother and uncle. Somehow she would convince them, because she must.

"All right, Kathy," she said very quietly, "I'll go with you. . . ."

Late in February 1778, a sentry at Valley Forge blinked his half-blinded eyes. It was a hard thing for him to do, because both his lashes and his brows were beaded with ice. The snow came driving down from the hills and stung his face. Cautiously he lifted his musket, and held it in readiness, the bayonet pointed toward the break between the ravines. He was almost sure he had seen something move over there. But then the white curtain of snow closed down again.

Yes. Something had moved. There was a large object ploughing through the snow. The sentry held his musket at readiness. He didn't aim it. There was no need to.

He knew perfectly well it wouldn't fire—not with all this fine snow ruining the priming.

The object came closer. He could make it out now. It was a sleigh, drawn by two fine, fat horses. He hadn't seen horses like that in a long time. Most of the horses at Valley Forge were already dead—of starvation, and of freezing.

He tried to get his blue, frozen jaws open to cry:

"Halt, who goes there?" But he couldn't. His face was too numb with the cold. So it was that Polly Knowles was upon him before she even saw him.

She drew up the sleigh and sat there staring at that scarecrow with a rifle. The man had on seven or eight suits of clothes, all of them in rags. His feet were wrapped in sacking, and he stood in his hat. He was thinner than any man is supposed to be and yet stay alive. His breath plumed out of his nostrils in wisps, like white smoke, and he stood there blinking his eyes.

He tried to say something, but a gust of coughing racked him. The tears came out of his eyes from the coughing and froze on his blue cheeks. He spat into the snow. His spittle made a dark splotch, like blood. Then Polly saw it was blood.

I won't cry, she thought, I won't! But if their sentries look like this, what must the rest of them be?

"Colonel Page?" she called out. "Colonel Ethan Page?"

The sentry pointed toward a group of huts.

"Thank you," Polly said, and drove on.

She found Ethan sitting in a sod hut, wrapped in a frayed blanket. He tried to stand up as she came in, but he couldn't. He looked like that sentry. No—worse. He hadn't on any boots and his little toe poked through the rags he'd wrapped his feet in. It was black.

He had on only his shirt and trousers under that blanket.

"Ethan," she whispered, "your clothes——"

"Sentries," he croaked. "They have to be warm. So we wrap up and lend 'em our things. That's where my boots are now. And my greatcoat."

"Oh, Ethan!" Polly wailed.

"Don't cry, Polly," Ethan croaked. "Going to win—if we get through this winter . . ."

"I've got food," Polly got out. "I'll go get it—it's outside in the sleigh . . ."

She came staggering in a moment later with an enormous ham. While Ethan watched her with famished eyes, she hacked great slices off it with his dagger, and toasted them over the smoky fire on a bayonet. Then she laid them on rough-cut slabs of bread and handed them to Ethan. She leaned back against the walls of the hut and watched him wolf them down, while she explained to him that she was visiting in Philadelphia, making no mention of Kathy.

It was surprising how much stronger his voice became when he had finished.

"Polly," he said, "dear little Polly. Did I ever tell you you were an angel?"

"No," Polly said. "You never told me that."

"How'd you do it?" Ethan said. "It's been snowing for four days. Where'd you get the stuff? What did you use for money?"

"You keep still and eat," Polly told him.

He did.

It's no good telling him that this is Uncle Peter's

money that bought these things. Or that I won't have any fine new dresses to attend the Tory balls because I spent the money on food and clothes and things for him. Look at him. Oh dear, look at him!

"Polly . . ."

"Yes, Ethan?"

"Would you—would you mind very much if I kissed you? Out of gratitude, I mean. I know you don't love me any more. Not after the way I treated you . . ."

"No, Ethan," Polly whispered, "I don't mind."

He stood up. Came to her. But before he released her, he felt the tears on her face.

"Please, Polly," he said, "don't cry."

"I can't help it," Polly said. "Look, I have more food in the sleigh—much more. If you'll just help me get it out . . ."

"Gladly," Ethan said.

But afterwards he stood in the hut staring at the mound of supplies.

"It isn't very much," he muttered.

It was actually enough to keep him for quite a while. Until the warm weather came, if he were careful. Polly stared at him. Then she read his thought.

"You mustn't, Ethan," she said. "You simply can't divide with the men! This would all be gone in a week, and then you'd starve afterwards anyhow . . ."

He smiled at her, crookedly.

"Polly," he said, "remember that time we went on a picnic and that hungry little mongrel came out of the woods and stood there watching us eat? We all fed him, remember, because we couldn't stand the look in his eyes. And these are human beings, Polly—men . . ."

"But, Ethan," Polly wailed, "I spent all the money I had! I don't think I can get any more . . ."

Ethan put his arm around her shoulders.

"It's all right, Polly," he said gently. "And thank you. Thank you so very much."

"But you'll die!" Polly sobbed. "I can't let you, Ethan! I just can't let you die!"

"I won't die. Not if there's any justice in the universe. I think we'll pull through this. I think the God Who loves the brave will bring us out of this wilderness just as He has brought us out of battles where by every tenet of military art we should have been massacred. You should know that, Polly. You're the bravest girl I've ever known—and the finest. . . ."

Polly looked at him. "Say it, Ethan," she thought. "You can now. There's nothing to prevent you. Not Kathy. She doesn't exist—not the Kathy you knew. You wouldn't know her now, Ethan. She isn't pretty any more—not even as pretty as I am. I feel so sorry for her. She's been a fool, but not wicked. You're free, Ethan—and I—I can't even tell you so. . . ."

"Come over to headquarters with me," Ethan said. "General Washington will want to see you . . ."

Polly bowed her head.

"All right, Ethan," she whispered.

General Washington's headquarters were in the little stone house of Mistress Deborah Hewes, just across the frozen Valley Creek. As they started out toward it, Polly saw Ethan limp.

"Ethan," she cried, "I nearly forgot. I brought you some boots and a new greatcoat—well, not exactly new —it belonged to my uncle. Please wait a minute, and I'll get them . . ."

Ethan waited. And when they started out again, for the first time in weeks his feet were warm. Except, of course, the frostbitten toes from which all feeling had forever gone.

Alexander Hamilton, now chief secretary to the General, showed them in. George Washington took Polly's hand, and stood there holding it a long time. All the terrible strain of holding up alone upon his broad shoulders—the burden of an entire nation—showed upon his face. It was lined, old. His mouth trembled a little.

"God bless you, Miss Knowles," he said, "for coming to our aid. If only we had a dozen like you in Congress . . ."

Looking at him, Polly wanted to cry. She had never seen so much sadness in one human face. Here was this man pledged to fight the finest army in the world, and left to do that task with no food, no clothing for his men, no ammunition, no money, no sources of supply. This Commander of a legion of dying specters, wind-whipped, frozen, starving, naked, so that even as she stood there Polly could hear beneath his window that dreadful chorus:

"No food—no rum—no clothes—I'm sick—I'm frozen!"

"General," Polly said, "do you think you can win, even now?"

Washington stood there looking at her a long time before he answered:

"Yes, Miss Knowles. We'll win—because we must."

He said it very calmly. His voice was low, even a little flat. But Polly felt something like goose-pimples all over her body at the sound of it. It was so majestic in its calm. So certain. And then she knew he was right.

They would win, and largely because of him. This big, ugly man with the bad teeth and the pock-marked face couldn't be beaten. He might know nothing of war; he might make every mistake in the military manuals, and invent a few to be added to that part of tactics which deals with errors to be avoided; but he was going to win.

He was because he would never know when he was beaten. He would come up off the ground a thousand times, and keep fighting, and every time he did the men who had deserted him from hunger and cold and fear and the suffering of their families would flock back to him because they loved him. He wasn't the kindest man alive. He would punish them cruelly, but always he tried to be just and they knew that. He was their great, stern father, who whipped his children to better them, believing truly it was for their own good.

And he was the only man who all those three years of hopelessness never wavered, whose faith was so great that it swayed the doubters, and triumphed over starvation, disease, hunger, the elements, and treachery. It was just, Polly realized, that harassed, tormented, reviled, bumbling, inept, he always managed to seem a little bit larger than life. Seem? That was not the word. He was. And nothing, not even his own blunders, would stand against the greatness of his soul. . . .

"Come, Miss Knowles," George Washington said, "I want to show you about the camp. I don't think you're the kind of young lady who faints or suffers with the vapors. What I'm going to show you is going to be bad to see, but I think you can bear up under it. Can you?"

"Yes," Polly said. "But why do you want me to see it, sir?"

"I'm going to send you on a mission. I want you to ride to Lancaster and acquaint the members of the Congress with what we're suffering here. I've written them a thousand times. So have Wayne, and the others. But they do nothing. I think you can convince them. I remember your spirit. Can I depend upon you, Miss Knowles?"

"Yes, sir," Polly said. "I'm at your command, General."

As they started that grim parade a big, handsome officer joined them. General Washington introduced him to Polly. His name was Anthony Wayne. Later his inspired, reckless valor would lead men to call him "Mad Anthony;" but even then Polly could see he was a man to remember. But there were other things to remember here. Ten minutes later, Polly was crying so hard she couldn't see, and the tears kept freezing on her face. She was brave, but she couldn't help but cry. They went into huts, and piles of rags stirred, became three, four, five men, huddled together trying to keep alive by sharing their bodily warmth. In others officers sat, clad in dressing gowns made of tattered blankets pinned together with thorns and splinters of animal bone. There were no horses. They were all dead, lying in frozen mounds under the snow.

In the filthy, smoky hut that served as a hospital, the surgeons were sawing off the frozen feet of soldiers, while the irons heated, waiting. Not more than one man in three survived that ordeal. Polly put her handkerchief to her nose to keep out the smell. Even cold as it was, the odor of gangrene, of unwashed flesh, of blood, stifled her.

They were putting the bodies in a shed now to keep until spring. The ground was too hard to dig graves into, and anyhow nobody had the strength.

"The scoundrels, the miserable scoundrels!" Anthony Wayne burst out, his big handsome face streaked with unashamed tears. "You know what's happening, Miss Polly? Our privateers have captured shiploads of hats and boots and clothing. There are hogsheads of boots mildewing in New York right now, because the men holding the letters of marque are holding them for a rise in price! And we have to saw off their poor frozen feet . . .

"I wrote the Clothier General to send me some of the shoes stored at York. You know what he wrote me, Miss Polly? That the Congress had given him no authorization for their distribution! They sent me a shipment of coats—'contract jobs'—which is a polite word for thievery. The first time these poor devils came in out of the snow, those coats wouldn't fit a ten-year-old boy. And I wanted bayonets—stored at Reading—and Dick Paters wrote me back that he couldn't send 'em because he'd just sent me the bloody coats and didn't want to be accused of partiality!"

He turned, his face working with rage, and faced General Washington.

"I tell you, General, you ought to let me take a few of my Pennsylvania boys, and raid York and Reading! I don't care whose side they say they're on, when they let us die like this by inches, shooting's too good for 'em!"

"Patience, Wayne," the General said. "That would

be mutiny. We'll have to try to do our best, within the law. . . ."

"It's a good thing," Ethan said, after they had left Anthony Wayne, "that he hasn't heard what happened to Nat Greene . . ."

"What was that, Colonel?"

"They had a supply of uniforms for his men. That was in December. They haven't come yet. The reason? Because they can't decide what kind of buttons to put on them!"

General Washington bowed his head. The gesture was eloquent enough. There was no need for words.

Ethan helped Polly up into the sleigh. Then he stood back, looking at her. General Washington took her hand, and kissed it. "We're depending upon you," he said.

"I'll do my best," Polly promised, and General Washington bowed and took his leave.

Polly lifted the whip. Then she put it back again in the socket.

"Come here, Ethan," she said.

Ethan came to her. She leaned out of the sleigh and kissed his cracked, frozen mouth. Then she straightened up, but her hands still rested on his shoulders.

" 'Bye, Ethan," she whispered.

"Polly," Ethan said. "What was that for?"

"Because I love you," Polly said simply. "I said I'd never tell you that again. But I'm not ashamed now. What is my little pride to be compared with what you're doing—with what all of you here are doing?"

"Polly, dearest——"

"No, Ethan. Don't say anything. If you—you don't come back, I'll have the memory of having known you, even this little. And it's a great honor, Ethan—to have known such a man as you . . ."

"I'll come back," Ethan growled. "I've so much to make up to you, Polly. So many years of neglect, so much blindness . . ."

Polly laid her fingers across his mouth.

"Don't say those things, my darling. I won't listen. Not now. Say them when this war is over and you've come back and know how you feel then. Tell me then, if you can . . ."

Then she kissed him once more, hard upon the mouth.

"Polly——" he began, but she brought her whip down across the horses' flanks and was off in a swirl of snow.

She went to Lancaster, as she had promised General Washington. The few sleepy members of Congress she could find listened to her politely, and promised to send aid. But they were too sleek, too fat, too warm, and wine-soaked, and comfortable. In two or three days, they forgot every word they'd said.

But up at Valley Forge, Captain Allan McLane managed to save the lives of the soldiers. The way he did it was very simple. He stole horses from the farmers, paying them in worthless continentals, and formed a cavalry troop. He took his wife's household and table linens and had them cut up to make breeches for his riders. They had beaver hats, but no coats or boots. And the temperature was ten above zero.

As soon as he learned what they were doing, Ethan begged to join that troop. He offered to resign his commission and serve as a simple trooper under McLane's command. But General Washington waived that offer and made him second-in-command though he outranked McLane.

Then they were off, whirling through the snow, to raid the mile-long trains of Quaker wagons bringing General Howe his supplies. The Quakers would have supplied Valley Forge as well, but they wanted gold, not continentals. And already people were using the phrase, "Not worth a continental," to express the very nadir of worthlessness.

Sometimes they had to shoot up the horse guards that Howe sent to protect his supplies. But nearly always they came back after that with the laden wagons, filled with food.

Even that was not enough, but it kept the men alive. And Polly Knowles came back again in March, with more boots and clothes and food, having pawned all her jewelry and sold her finer dresses to pay for them.

But it was not enough. Nothing was enough. By March, three thousand men had deserted to the British. Another four thousand were unfit for duty from utter lack of clothes and shoes. The Ninth Pennsylvania now consisted of two officers with no privates to command.

"Yet we shall endure," Ethan Page wrote to Polly Knowles, "because what we fight for is indestructible. Though we, through our bodies' feebleness, succumb to hunger and to cold; though some of us fall prey to littleness of heart and the weakness of our souls and turn traitor, freedom cannot be destroyed. It may be that we shall be crushed here in the valley of our anguish; but should we fail, afterwards our sons shall rise up; and their sons after them, if need be; generation upon generation until the last visage of despotism shall have vanished from the earth. For this is the meaning of America: that everywhere men shall stand up tall in liberty, proud in human dignity; this we have written with our blood upon the snows at Valley Forge: that until, which God forbid, she be destroyed, America shall remain the implacable foe of tyranny in all ages, anywhere upon the earth . . .

"And America shall not be vanquished, for she is liberty's body; and freedom is her soul . . ."

Polly wept, reading these words. But her tears were tears of pride.

They did endure. And Polly endured with them. She and Kathy were able to remain in Philadelphia all winter living at a respectable boarding house for young women—for to have stayed with friends would have raised too many questions. As it was, because of the upheaval of war, and the trouble which had robbed them of the supervision of their father, Polly and Kathy enjoyed a certain amount of freedom. Polly had tried to comfort her mother by hinting that things were less dark than they appeared; but Uncle Peter had simply cut them both off from any consideration as members of the family. As for her father, they were trying to keep the news of Kathy's disgrace from him—and of Polly's almost equally disgraceful behavior, in their eyes, of aiding and abetting her.

But Polly got a sum of money from her father for the journey, so sunk in his depression of mind and weakness of body that he failed even to ask what she wanted it for. And Cecil, of course, supplied his secret bride with funds.

But Polly was sick of it all: the lies, the deceptions, concealing Kathy's absences from the good widow who ran the boarding house for working girls without families. Fortunately this was easy to do, because the Widow Phewett was very old, remarkably deaf, and retired at sunset. To write letters to her mother was a kind of torture. If only Kathy would let her tell the truth! Surely all the money in the world was not worth the pain this deception was causing! But Kathy would not relent. So Polly went on, seeing Ethan when she could, concealing the real facts from him as well. . . .

On the sixth of May, Polly stood beside Ethan and watched a parade. It was led by a fat, ugly little General she had never seen before. Behind him, the troops marched at a running pace, each man with a white flower in his hat, or pinned in his hair if he didn't have a hat. They were something to see. They had patched their rags as best they could, but they still fluttered at knee and seat and elbow in splendid tatters. Miracle of miracles, not one of them was out of step.

Polly turned to Ethan, her eyes filled with amazement at the sight.

"Credit Von Steuben for that," Ethan smiled. "The fat little man who's leading them, I mean. Beaumarchais sent him over to train us. He didn't dare send a Frenchman, then. But he couldn't have chosen a better man. They're soldiers now, Polly; I don't think they'll ever panic again . . ."

"Which one is De La Fayette?" Polly asked.

"You would ask that," Ethan grinned. "All the women do. There he is, over there with General Washington and Alexander Hamilton . . ."

Polly stared quite openly at the handsome boy in the pigskin boots and the flashing spurs and the beautifully tailored uniform the cost of which would have fed a company for a month. Then she looked at General Washington, and what she saw in his face moved her. All that old warrior's hunger for a son melted into the pride and tenderness that glowed in his gray eyes as he gazed upon this boy he couldn't even talk to unless Hamilton, who had learned his French at his mother's knee, interpreted for them.

Polly turned her gaze once more upon the French boy with the long nose and red hair and blue eyes full of worship for Washington, for America, and for liberty. Her gaze was soft. Ethan didn't mind. This romantic youth seemed to appeal to all women. It was not too much to say that neither Washington nor America nor liberty would have stood the chance they now had of coming into full being without that boy called Marie Joseph Paul Yves Roche Gilbert du Motier, Marquis de la Fayette. . . .

Behind them, now, the Valley Creek was sparkling in the sun. The grass was green. Only in the places where the sunlight couldn't reach was there any snow left. And little rivulets of water ran down from the edges of each grayish mound. Polly had a feeling that there never had been before, or never would be again, a spring like this one. After that frozen hell, it was life again; after death, resurrection. . . .

There was food again now in God's own plenty. And there were flagons of wine. La Fayette had bought the wine. They had something to celebrate all right. France had come to their aid—openly at long last. She had declared war on England. They had as an ally now the second-biggest fleet in the world, the biggest standing army, the richest nation in Europe. It was something. Munitions and supplies had trickled in from France since 1777; now they were going to swell into a flood. And soldiers, too, trained soldiers to help them shoot the lobsterbacks.

It was something. Just thinking about it was enough to make a man drunken. And on top of that, they had wine.

They split the sky open with their cheering. The cannon jumped and thundered, bellowing salutes. They wasted precious ammunition firing off their muskets in the air. And when George Washington rode by on his big white stallion, splendid in his regimentals, they blasted sound out of existence by the sheer torrential volume of their noise.

Polly looked at Ethan out of the corner of her eye. There was spring in her heart, too; inside her veins, a sound like singing. Her brown eyes were soft with adoration. Ethan was as thin as a skeleton. He would never walk again without a limp. They had taken two toes off one foot, and one off the other. She'd never dance with him again. And he did so love to dance! she wailed inside her heart.

"I hear Howe's resigned," Ethan said.

"Yes," Polly said, "he has."

"Don't understand that Britisher," Ethan said. "He had sixteen thousand foot, and three thousand horse, and yet he sat around Philadelphia and did nothing. He could have carried us in five minutes any time he wanted to. He must have known how bad off we were, he had enough of our deserters to tell him. No food, little ammunition, thirty-five hundred frozen, starving, barebacked devils—heck, Polly, half our guns wouldn't have fired . . .

"And now, at the news that the French are coming

—he quits cold! Now—long before a single Frogeater has arrived . . ."

"They're going to give a farewell ball in his honor," Polly said tartly. She was annoyed because Ethan had broken into her tender thoughts; because he had been unable to sense her mood and fall into it; that he was able to think of war and fighting on such a day. "I'm going to attend it, Ethan."

"Good," Ethan said. "I'm glad you're having fun, Polly. And that's the answer, isn't it, to the riddle of Sir William Howe? Too many distractions. Who the devil wanted to go marching through the snow when he could sit in a nice warm house in Philly, drink brandy sours, and stroke Mrs. Loring's lily-white hand? Come to think of it, we rebels ought to erect a monument to Mrs. Loring—for defeating in the drawing room a man we couldn't whip in the field!"

"Yes," Polly said bitterly, "to her—and to others—like Kathy, for instance."

Ethan stared at her.

"I'm sorry," Polly said quickly, "that was ill of me, Ethan. Kathy—Kathy has never meant anyone harm . . ."

"Of course not," Ethan said calmly. "Kathy can no more help having her little flirtations than she can help breathing air. And her flirtations have always been harmless. We're going to win now, and after we do . . ."

He didn't finish the sentence. Polly waited, holding her breath. She had to know now, how he felt. All those months at Valley Forge, he had never before mentioned Kathy—not even once. I, Polly thought sadly, can keep still and he'll turn to me after he finds that Kathy is married. But I don't want him like that!

I don't want to be second choice. I want to be loved for myself alone. Then she saw that Ethan wasn't going to finish his thought. And she had to know, she had to . . .

"You'll come back to Kathy when it's done?" she said. "But I know that already, Ethan . . ."

Ethan turned to her and caught her by both her arms.

"When I come back," he said quietly, "it will not be to Kathy, Polly. It was you who told me to wait, remember? I had no need for waiting. That I now remember Kathy with kindness is only proof that I am free of her . . ."

Polly moved suddenly, jerking herself free of his grip.

"I wish I could believe that!" she said; then, "Ah yes, Ethan—I shall go to that ball!"

The Mischianza Ball, which Major John André designed in honor of Sir William Howe, was very fine. Polly went in a borrowed dress, a castoff of Kathy's that ordinarily she would have been ashamed to wear. But now she wore it proudly. Knowing what she had done with her dresses and her jewels, this faded, worn dress was a robe of honor. Her pride enveloped it, made it fine.

It showed in her bearing, that pride. She carried her head a little higher, and something like fire blazed in the depths of her dark eyes.

John André saw these things. There were dozens of girls there far prettier than Polly. But he couldn't take his eyes off her.

"Who the devil is that one, Cecil?" he said to Major Fitzgerald, who had just come up with Kathy on his arm.

"My sister," Kathy said. "Miss Polly Knowles—and an ardent rebel, Major André."

"You've got to present me, old boy!" John André laughed. "Gad, what a striking creature! Not pretty, really, but interesting—deuced interesting . . . D'you know, Miss Knowles, your sister looks as though were she to touch you, you'd be jolly well set afire."

"I'd never noticed," Kathy said airily.

"Well, you've always been a little unjust to her as I've often told you," Cecil said dryly. "Excuse us, won't you? Come along, John; I shall be glad to present you . . ."

Polly drew herself up stiffly and looked at John André with grave eyes. But there were two things concerning André about which even his brother officers were in unanimous agreement: he was the handsomest man in the entire British Army; and he could charm a bird out of a tree. . . .

"Oh, I say, Miss Knowles," he laughed, "don't be so formidable! I know of your opinions; and I think you're perfectly entitled to them. I don't propose to discuss either war or politics with you. All I'm asking for now is a dance, not General Washington's head!"

In spite of herself, Polly had to smile. It was easy to smile at John André. And why not? she thought. Am I to spend my life dreaming of a man who cannot forget my sister, and who will never really love me? Besides, this boy is nice. English or not, he's very nice. . . .

"Very well, Major André," she said. "I'll dance with you. . ."

"Thank you so very much," John André said. "D'you know, that had you refused, I'd have been the un-happiest man alive?"

"Why?" Polly said as they swirled away to the music.

"Your face. Odd sort of face. Rather haunting. Not beautiful in the conventional sense, but so very alive—the kind a chap doesn't forget. Exciting is the word I mean, perhaps. But more than that—provocative, alluring—— What's behind that face, Miss Knowles? What goes on beyond those great and searching eyes?"

"Searching?" Polly said.

"Yes, yes! I have the feeling that they can see right through one; that sham and pretense are of no service against them. Eyes like yours have measured many men, I think, and found them all wanting . . ."

"I haven't found you wanting—yet," Polly said.

"God forbid you ever do," John André whispered, and Polly had the feeling that he meant every word he said.

Some hours later, she stood with him on the balcony and watched the fireworks. She was troubled. Ethan had sworn he'd come back to her, and yet . . .

What's wrong with me? she thought. I like him. He's English—and the enemy of my country—Ethan's enemy, but I like him. Am I like Kathy too? Is it something in our blood? But he's so nice, so gay—so handsome. So wonderfully handsome. The best-looking boy I've ever seen in my whole life—ever so much better-looking than——

Than Ethan. That was what she had been about to think. And now she had thought it, shaping the words in the darkness of her mind.

"Take me back inside now, Major," she whispered.

"No, wait!" John André laughed. "There're going to be more—even better ones. Look—there they go now!"

The rockets streamed heavenward. The *feu d'artifice*

burst in matchless brilliance, painting vivid Chinese fountains, etched in many-colored fire against the velvet sky.

But Polly stiffened, catching André's arm. Those weren't fireworks. Not that sound. Death-deep, shaking the very earth. She looked around her. The other watchers on the balcony were frozen too, their faces strained with listening.

"Those aren't fireworks," she said to Major André.

"I think they are," he smiled. "A very special type, perhaps. . . ."

He was right. They were a special type. They were Allan McLane's and Ethan Page's contributions to the festivities. Camp kettles filled with gunpowder don't make pretty lights in the sky. But what they did to the British outpost was a caution.

On June eighteenth, 1778, the British evacuated Philadelphia and started the march back to New York. Washington followed them. On the twenty-eighth, in the blinding heat of a day more than a hundred in the shade, he caught up with them. If he had used cavalry, he would have cut their clumsy wagon train to pieces. But Washington never learned what to do with cavalry. His failure to employ horsemen had cost him the battle of Long Island. The slaughter at Paoli was due to sending out foot soldiers as scouts when he should have used hard-riding troopers. Less than a week ago now, he had almost lost De La Fayette by sending him out to scout with infantry across the Schuylkill. But Washington's density in the department of military tactics was as monumental as the rest of the man.

So Allan McLane and Ethan Page had to sit there

with their troopers and swear, while Charles Lee led
the infantry forward. On their flank, Count Casimir
Pulaski was on the verge of tears, cursing softly in
French and German and Polish, while his crack cavalry-
men held their nervous mounts hard, the horses pawing
the earth and snorting.

Then Lee came boiling back in full retreat and Ethan
turned to McLane.

"We're done," they said. "They'll chase us clear back
to Philly and beyond . . ."

Hamilton was crying, swearing that Lee had turned
traitor; and every man there was in black despair—
every man except three.

Ethan looked at McLane, waiting for him to signal
the retreat. The signal never came. Ethan Page had
reckoned without those three: Mad Anthony Wayne
who'd seen "No Flint" Grey torture his troops to death
with sword's edge and bayonet even after they had surrendered at Paoli, and who wasn't going to run any
more, not even if the devil had appeared out of hell
leading a legion of fiends; Baron von Steuben, who had
made soldiers out of those raw farmers, and who now
wheeled them into line with a barrage of shouted orders,
as perfectly as though they'd been soldiers all their lives
—without using his riding crop or the flat of his sword
or anything at all except his men's unshakable con-
fidence in his leadership; and the third and greatest of
all—George Washington.

He had made mistakes, but he was big enough to
survive them. After he had relieved Lee, knowing him
finally for the weakling and the fool he was, George
Washington spurred into battle.

Ethan gave one look at him, and knew they were going to win.

"I'm going with him!" he shouted to McLane. "I'm going to cover the General!"

Then he was off, flying beside the big man on the magnificent white horse. Washington was everywhere at once, shouting orders, wheeling regiments back into line, changing officers, covering the whole battlefield. To Ethan it seemed that the white charger's hoofs struck fire, and that the god of war himself sat like a rock in that saddle, gigantic above the roar of battle, riding until the stallion's eyes were redder than the blood of the dying, his great flanks dripping sweat, and ropes of foam flecking backward as he tore great clods up from the earth each time his hoofs dug in.

Ethan was hard put to keep up with his Commander. He didn't even hear the musket balls whining around him, or the crash and thunder of the cannon. Then he pulled up his black stallion so hard the beast reared, and all his breath stopped somewhere down in his throat; his breath and his heart and his life in that long, slow moment while General Washington's white charger somersaulted head over heels, the sound his neck made breaking clear above the crack of musketry, and the General going down with him, caught in the thrashing of giant hoofs.

Then George Washington leaped free, and Ethan could breathe again.

The Commander in Chief stood there trembling, while every marksman in the British line aimed and fired at him, the balls whistling their song of death. But the General did not move. He stood there, tears in his eyes, looking down at that noble beast who had carried him through so many battles without a scratch, until the great stallion stiffened his mighty limbs, shuddered, and died.

Then, very slowly, the General turned.

"Billy!" he called. "Bring me the chestnut mare!"

Ethan saw Bill Lee, Washington's Negro servant, coming out through that hail of death, leading the mare. Billy didn't think about the bullets any more than anyone who was with Washington ever did. They knew, without knowing how they knew, that death could not come nigh this man.

The General mounted. And every man in that ragged army ripped out a cheer.

The British were done, then; and they knew it. Washington charged on, with Ethan covering his flank, and the men loosed cheer after cheer. There was no stopping them after that—not with George Washington setting their hearts on fire, and Wayne slashing in like a madman, and old Von Steuben directing them so that they did everything right, cross fire, infiltration, bayonet work, turning back into line every time they were driven back instead of flying away in a panic; and cool Nat Greene, who'd never forgotten Concord, emptied more than half the British officers from their saddles with his sharpshooters placed behind trees. . . .

So they won Monmouth, which should have been a defeat, against overwhelmingly superior numbers. But for Washington's failure to send out cavalry to smash those baggage wagons, they could have destroyed Sir Henry Clinton's army.

It was a good thing he did not, though. Because in many of the wagons, the British officers had taken along their tenderest prizes of war—like Mrs. Loring. Like Kathy Knowles. And Polly rode along with her.

On that journey home, Polly was filled with anxiety because she had had no word from home in weeks. The movement of the troops had completely disrupted the mails. When they reached New York at last, Polly went at once to see her parents. Kathy didn't go. She knew that she wouldn't be welcome.

But when Polly reached the house, one look at the face of the maid who opened the door convinced her that her worries had been justified.

"Papa?" she whispered.

"Two weeks ago, God rest his soul," the maid said gently. "Your poor mama's been grieving herself sick ever since she came back from the funeral. You better go see her."

Polly found her mother alone. Gertrude gave one look at her daughter and burst into bitter tears.

"Your papa," she got out. "Ach, Polly, your poor, poor papa!"

And Polly stood there, holding her mother. She was surprised she couldn't cry—that she felt no pain, nothing at all except a vast, all-pervading loneliness.

Poor papa, she thought. He was a good man. And she didn't realize then how fine a thing that was, and of how few men it could be said.

But when Patrick Knowles' will was read, Polly found to her surprise that her father had left the bulk of his fortune to her as well as the control of his business under the guidance of her uncle, with the provision that she take care of her mother and Kathy.

To Kathy he left also a considerable dowry, stating

that Kathy's frivolity of temper and lack of foresight being such as they were, it would be foolish to let her control her own monies, since she needed the firm guidance that his younger daughter, and later, he hoped, a good husband, would provide.

Hearing this, Polly was glad. It showed how well Patrick Knowles had known his children—and conceivably, it might free Kathy from her promise to Cecil. With this dowry, they might not have to depend upon his father's good will. . . .

But when she tried to find her sister, Kathy had disappeared. She and Cecil were both gone from New York—where, not even his fellow officers knew.

That troubled Polly. Then it came to her that Kathy really had no immediate need for the money—not now. And that there might be other places like Valley Forge, other times she could help Ethan—and the cause.

Patrick Knowles had done a fine thing for her. Without knowing it, he had provided a daughter of the Republic with the sinews of war—money.

CHAPTER 8

"Polly," John André said, "I'm going away. I'm not supposed to tell anyone, but I had to tell you . . ."

"Why?" Polly said.

"Because I'm going on a confidential mission. If I succeed, Sir Henry Clinton has promised that I shall be knighted . . ."

"And if you fail?" Polly whispered.

"I shall die," John André said.

"Oh," Polly murmured. She had again that feeling of being caught between two fires. In the nearly three years since she had met young John André at Sir William Howe's farewell ball in Philadelphia and this bright September day of 1780, she had had that feeling many times. She liked John André. She liked everything about him—the way he held her hand, and whispered outrageous nonsense into her ear, and even—rarely—tried to kiss her. And, to be perfectly honest about it, occasionally succeeded. There had even been times when the feeling she had for him had been dangerously greater than liking. Then she remembered Ethan—how he'd stood up through last winter at Morristown, the real Golgotha of the Revolution, ten times worse than Valley Forge—and she drew back. Ethan's quiet courage made even this light and pleasant dalliance with André seem shameful to her.

She looked at André now, sitting there in her office, waiting for her to speak.

"Aren't you going to say anything, Polly?" André said.

"No, John. I—I should be very sorry if you were killed. I like you very much. But, if you succeed, you'll help my country to be defeated, and I should be sorry for that, too. . . ."

John André took a golden snuffbox from his pocket, and applied a pinch to his nostril. Then he whipped out a lace handkerchief from his breast pocket and stifled a sneeze. Polly had the impression that she had seen something fall to the floor out of the handkerchief, but André was talking again, so she forgot it.

"You're a marvel, Polly," he said. "Don't think I've ever heard of a woman running an importing business before . . ."

"I don't run it—or rather I do, but I'm not supposed to. I own it, but my uncle Peter has always run it for me. However, this spring, when he and my mother decided to get married, I took over for three weeks so that they could go away on a honeymoon. Uncle Peter was so pleased with the way I managed things that he's left them more and more in my hands ever since. He says that I keep far better books than he does . . ."

"I don't doubt it. You've a head on your shoulders, Polly. Dear Polly—if I should become Sir John André——"

Polly stopped him with a lifted hand.

"Don't, John," she said. "We've been friends—though I'll admit there've been times that I forgot what color coat you wore. Let's keep it like that, shall we?"

"Right," John André said. "I'm sorry, Polly." He

bent over her hand. Then he straightened up, and looked full into her eyes.

"Remember, Polly," he said quietly, "the fact that whatever there was between us has been no more was your fault, not mine. It could have been much—much more. . . ."

It was very still in the office after he had gone. Polly didn't move. There was warfare in her soul. He is so fine, she thought, so gentle and so fine. And Ethan is so good and brave . . . Oh God, I—— Then she saw the little folded piece of paper on the floor.

She picked it up, opened it. She knew she shouldn't; but she was a woman, and already her nostrils had caught the faint scent of perfume that clung to it.

> Dear John [*she read*]. Dear, dear John. You're an angel to oblige me. I shan't trouble you too much, though. My needs will be satisfied by 1 pair stockings, 4 pair white thread, 1 pair black satin, 2 caps, 1 very light coat. Trusting I shall hear from you again soon—or better yet, even see you, I remain,
>
> Devotedly yours,
> Peggy Shippen Arnold.

Polly was surprised at how sharp the stab of pain that went through her was. She knew Peggy Shippen. Kathy and Peggy had been the best of friends in Philadelphia. If anything, Peggy was more of a flirt than Kathy. Polly remembered how astonished everyone had been when Major General Benedict Arnold, that finest of the American Army's fighting men, had married so outspoken a Tory as Peggy in April of 1779.

What kind of a woman is she, Polly thought angrily, that she has another man besides her husband buy her stockings? Oh yes, John André, you're charming all right! I wonder how many other women have found you so.

Then she tore the letter into bits and threw it into the wastebasket. Which was a mistake. She should have gotten that letter to Aaron Burr, Chief of the American Secret Service. Burr would have known how to read it, or would have soon learned that 2 caps were two heavy cannon, 1 very light coat, a battalion of dragoons, 4 pair white thread were in sly Peggy's code four regiments of light infantry. Poor, disappointed, reviled, falsely maligned Benedict Arnold was being driven into treason by his country's ingratitude and the wiles of the scheming woman he was fool enough to love. . . .

She bent her head down and was about to give vent to the blessed relief of tears when a heavy footstep jerked her to attention.

Daniel Page stood there, looking at her curiously.

"What's the matter, Polly?" he said gently.

"Nothing, sir," Polly said tiredly, "nothing at all. . . ."

Daniel Page came closer. His face was worn and tired, but his eyes were proud still.

"You've made the arrangements?" he whispered.

"Yes, sir," Polly said. "The same as usual, Captain Hym will put the supplies ashore at the usual place day after tomorrow. Get word to Ethan to meet him there . . ."

"God bless you, Polly!" Dan Page said with feeling. "There must be many a lad beside my Ethan——"

He stopped and looked at her.

"You can trust this Captain Hym?"

"He's loyal to the core," Polly said. "He lost his leg serving under John Paul Jones on the *Bonhomme Richard*. I had a hard time getting him to take command of the *Trudy*. It wasn't until I told him what we were really doing that he consented . . ."

"Good!" Dan Page said. "You've relieved my mind. Polly, I have to admit I was worried about you. That young British officer—André—a fine broth of a lad; I was beginning to fear . . ."

"That I was falling in love with him?" Polly said. "And that if I were, I might betray our organization?"

"No—you're too fine for that, Polly. My concern was —more personal. I want to see my boy happy, Polly. And I've always wanted a daughter—the right kind of a daughter——"

"Don't you think," Polly interrupted, "that Ethan should have something to say about that?"

"Ethan's very fond of you," Dan Page said.

"I know," Polly sighed, "but not fond enough, Mr. Page. I'm tired of wearing my heart on my sleeve. And John André has nothing to do with this. I'm not interested in him, either. I have no further interest in any man . . ."

"I'm sorry to hear you say that, Polly," Dan Page said.

How disinterested she was in John André was proved by the events. For a few days later, three professional skulkers, highway robbers, caught John André near Pleasantville, New York. He had disobeyed Sir Henry Clinton's orders and dressed in civilian clothes at Peggy Arnold's suggestion. And when the three bandits searched him, looking for gold, they found the map of

West Point in his boots and a pass signed by Benedict Arnold in his pocket. If he had had any gold, John Paulding and David Williams and Isaac van Wart would have let him go. But he didn't. So they turned him over to Colonel Jameson at North Castle and collected a fat reward. And Colonel Jameson in his sweet innocence sent a note to Benedict Arnold, saying he'd caught a spy with a pass forged with Arnold's name . . .

So Arnold got away, rowing out to the well-named *Vulture* in Haverstraw Bay. But they hanged John André, on a beautiful autumn morning, to the tune of fifers playing the "Blue Bird." Even the members of that military court wept to see him die. Hamilton had to hold La Fayette up. The little Marquis was so overcome he couldn't stand. And sobbing women by the dozens walked past that body clad in the dazzling white and green uniform they had given him, with the hair so carefully clubbed and powdered, and dropped wild daisies upon him and laurel. For everyone loved John André, that beautiful young man who died honorably for his cause.

When they told Polly Knowles of it, she cried three whole nights and days. Which proved how disinterested she was in him.

On New Year's Day of 1781, Ethan Page sat with his head bowed over his supper. I'm done, he thought. Finished. I could take everything but this . . . Two letters since September. And both of them penned in ice water. "I hope you are well. I am well and content . . ." What's happened to her? Has she, like Kathy before her, been enchanted by a scarlet coat? You'd think I were a blasted stranger! I've had enough. I feel exactly like those soldiers out there. I could howl, mutiny, desert . . .

He looked out of the window of the headquarters, and back at Anthony Wayne, to whom he was now assigned.

" 'Tis a bad business, Tony," he said. "The men are in an ugly mood . . ."

"I know," Wayne said.

It was snowing as usual, there at Mont Kemble, New Jersey. And outside of headquarters the men of the American Army, still half naked and uniformless and frozen after six years of broken promises by the Congress, wandered about and growled curses and stared up at the dull, gray sky.

"I gave 'em all an extra ration of rum after supper," Wayne said to Ethan. "Doesn't appear to have helped their spirits . . ."

"It's the fault of those thrice-blasted dunderheads in Congress," Ethan growled. "Today they sent recruiters into camp and gave twenty-five dollars in hard cash to the six-month militiamen. And our veterans haven't been paid in months—Tony! How many more Valley Forges and Morristowns do they think we can stand?"

"I don't know," Wayne muttered. "Another thing, Page, these troops of mine enlisted for three years or the duration. The three years are up today. And they're in a mood to say to hell with the duration. . . ."

And so am I, Ethan thought. If I could only see Polly—ask her . . .

Several other officers came into the room.

"Break out the punch bowls, boys!" Mad Anthony called. "We're going to have ourselves a party!"

But not even the grog helped Ethan's mood. It made

his thoughts run slower, that was all. It didn't make them any less black. He didn't even listen to the songs and the jokes. Before that dancing fire the room rocked with laughter. But Ethan didn't feel like laughing. He had never felt less like laughing in all his life.

A man should have something to go home to. A house of his own. A woman in it. A woman who loves him. But it's been too long. Six years. What else could I expect?

I'm crazy. She hasn't said anything like that. But those last two letters—why, those letters made the toes they cut off ache again! I could ask Tony—he'd give me a furlough . . . Maybe I could disguise myself and sneak into New York . . . "Good Lord! What's that?"

That was the sound of rifles being fired off into the air, and the howls of the ragged scarecrows gathered around headquarters. Ethan rushed to the door. Tony Wayne was just behind him.

Skyrockets were going up, lighting the night sky. By their light they saw the men rushing around, shooting off their guns, yelling, dragging out the dray horses and hitching them to the caissons.

Wayne rushed back and got his pistols. Then he and Ethan and the others marched out and were surrounded in an instant by thirteen hundred raging men.

Ethan drew his sword, smashed at them with the flat of the blade. The other officers were cursing at them, ordering them back to their huts.

"Cut out the rough stuff, Eth," one of the mutineers growled. "We don't be a-aiming to hurt you."

Ethan recognized the man. This gaunt scarecrow, grown bent and old in service, had been with him since old Put had made him a Colonel—had fought with him before that at Concord, had been one of the heroes of Breed's Hill. Ethan's sword came down limply to his side. You couldn't beat that kind of man. You couldn't kick him around. Not a man like that.

Wayne was screaming curses and pointing his cocked pistol at the mutineers. But he didn't fire. He couldn't. These were his beloved Pennsylvanians. He couldn't shoot them, any more than Ethan could strike his men. They circled him with bayonets like men keeping a tiger at bay. Some of them fired over his head.

Wayne dropped his pistols and jerked open his coat.

"If you mean to kill me," he roared, "here's my breast!"

Ethan laughed, but it was sad laughter. This was no time for silly heroics, and Tony should have known better.

One of the soldiers stepped out of line.

"General," he said. "We love you; we respect you. We'd follow you through hell and you know it. If the lobsterbacks was to show up right now we'd fight 'em right behind you and whip the daylights out of 'em, too.

"But we been fighting three years. Ain't given you much cause for complaint, neither. Some of our friends was butchered at Paoli, some of us is lame from the freezing and the British balls. And we ain't been paid. We're out to git what we deserve—or else we be a-going back to our wives and little ones. But right now, Gen'l, we aim to march on Philly and make Congress git a move on and ain't neither you, or old Eth Page, or the devil himself a-goin' to stop us!"

They shouted then, cheered. The horses pawed the snowy ground. The camp women screeched curses, spat at Tony Wayne. The caissons groaned and moved off. The men surged forward through the snow.

Mad Anthony Wayne ran toward the quarters of his light-horse brigade. He and Ethan and the others roused them out, and a few troops of still loyal infantry. Then they took the high footpath over the hills and cut the mutineers off before Elizabeth. They'd dragged some howitzers with them.

Mad Anthony stood in his stirrups waving his saber.

"Damn you, if you pass me, you'll pass me dead!" he roared.

The men plunged on. Tony Wayne turned. There were tears in his eyes.

"Fire on them," he half whispered.

The howitzers bucked and thundered, throwing grape. The light-horse surrounded the mutineers, slashing with espantoons. The men began to fall back.

"Shoot low!" Ethan was crying. "Damn your souls, shoot low—wing them boys! Shoot for their legs!"

He couldn't see. His eyes were blinded. He was crying and he didn't care who knew he was crying. He'd fought with these game, tattered devils for six years, and now he was having to kill them.

He saw the man who had spoken to him in camp go down, a musket ball through his guts. That was too much. He jerked out his big horse pistol and put the muzzle into his mouth. It missed fire. The next minute Tony Wayne smashed it out of his hand with his saber.

"Don't be a damned fool, Eth! We've got to do this!" he said.

It was over in minutes after that. Ethan Page went back to his quarters and lay down on his little bunk. The next morning, a little before dawn, he went outside and saddled his horse. Then he rode away from camp.

Ethan Page, after six long years of faithful service, was deserting the American Army.

The knock, when it came, was so faint that Polly wasn't sure she heard it. She had been asleep, but a moment ago, something had awakened her. She lay there in her bed, listening, unsure whether she had dreamed or heard that sound. It came again. Polly sat up.

"Who's there?" she called, trying to keep the tremble out of her voice.

"It's me," the whisper came back through the heavy door. "Kathy—in heaven's name let me in . . ."

Polly swung her feet down over the side of the bed. The floor was icy, but she couldn't find her slippers in the dark. She raced to the door, threw it open.

"Polly," Kathy whispered. "Please, Polly . . ."

"Come in," Polly said. She went over to the little table by her bed, and picked up the candle that burned there as a night light, sitting upright on a saucer that floated in a pan of water. That was because unwatched candles were dangerous. They had a way of falling over and setting things afire. In the Colonies people always floated their night lights on water as a precaution.

After she had lighted the big candles in the candelabra, she turned back to Kathy. Her sister's shawl and cloak were crusted with snow. There was snow in her lashes, in her hair. Her lips were blue. She was shaking.

"Let's go downstairs," Polly said. "Terrence has probably kept the fire going. You look half frozen."

"Polly," Kathy began; then stopped. "All right," she whispered, "let's go downstairs . . ."

The fire in the big fireplace was low, but it wasn't burned down too much to catch up again. Polly poked at it, added a log or two. It blazed up, pouring warmth into the room.

"Here," Polly said, "let me have your things. I'll hang them by the chimney to dry . . ."

"Thank you," Kathy murmured.

The fire was leaping now. Polly could see her sister clearly now. Kathy wasn't nice to look at now. Not any more. Polly could hardly keep from showing how shocked she was at the change in her sister in those three years since they had returned from Philadelphia. There were bluish hollows beneath her cheekbones. Her eyes were sunken, ringed with circles. And they were feverishly bright. She'd tried to conceal what had happened to her complexion by painting her face like an actress. She had done it badly. The splotches of rouge on her cheeks were garish in the firelight. Her mouth was messy with red lip salve.

She was thin. Polly had never seen her so thin. Her arms were like willow stems, her neck scarcely a single hand span.

"Kathy," Polly said, "you are in trouble, aren't you?"

"Yes," Kathy whispered. "It's—it's Cecil—he's left me, Polly!"

"Left you?" Polly cried. "Why, Kathy?"

"I—I don't know! We were away—in Canada—he was on some secret mission. We went from one place to another. Many times I wasn't well, and Cecil would be impatient. Then yesterday, when we got back to New

York, he found out that his father had died and he was ordered back to England . . ."

She bent her head and started crying, suddenly.

"I was overjoyed!" she wept. "Even though I had just heard about poor papa, I couldn't be too sad. I was the wife of the Sixth Earl of Breedingsford, titled, rich! Then Cecil told me—oh, Polly, I——"

"What did he tell you?" Polly asked grimly.

"That he had no intention of taking me back to England! That he was sick of me—that he couldn't risk jeopardizing his position with such a wife as I! Then he packed up and went down to the Officers' Quarters on Twenty-eighth Street . . ."

"And you?" Polly said gently.

"I walked about in the snow for hours. Then I decided that I'd better come to you. I had heard, too, about Mama's marriage to Uncle Peter, and that they had gone to Jamaica to escape the cold. They don't live here, do they, Polly? Why wouldn't you go to live with them? I understand that Mama is quite put out about it . . ."

"I wanted to be alone," Polly said. "I'm of age, and my own mistress. Besides, Uncle Peter and I don't agree on anything but business. I think he still suspects me of being slightly wicked . . . But I'd better get you something hot to drink. You're blue with cold."

"Yes," Kathy whispered. "I'd like a rum fustian, Polly. Or would that be too much trouble?"

"No," Polly said gently, "it won't be any trouble, Kathy."

She put the loggerhead in the fire to heat it. Then she went into the pantry and got the eggs, sugar and nutmeg. From the wine closet she took beer, sherry, and gin. She stirred them all together in a pitcher, using the red-hot poker to heat the mixture. Called fustian or imitation because there wasn't any rum in it, rum fustian was a drink to wake the dead.

After the first sip, she could see Kathy brighten. She had stopped crying now. After she had downed half of it, she wasn't shaking any more.

She put the pewter mug down on the table.

"Polly," she whispered. "Polly, what am I going to do?"

"You," Polly said firmly, "are going to bed now. And you're going to stay there tomorrow—all day—while I go down and have a talk with Cecil."

Kathy stood up.

"Oh, Polly," she wept, "you're so good!" Then impulsively she threw both her arms about her sister.

Polly put up her hand and stroked Kathy's bright hair. Then gently she took Kathy by the arm.

"Come," she said, "I'll put you to bed now."

First thing in the morning, she came out of the house and got into the sleigh that Terrence had brought around. Then she drove very rapidly uptown until she came to the house on Twenty-eighth Street where Cecil Fitzgerald was quartered.

She had little difficulty in seeing him. One of the younger officers announced her. From where she stood at the foot of the stairs she could hear him.

"Yes. Another one. Deuced pretty, too. Rather a bit of a gentlewoman, too, I'd say from her dress. You'll see her? Thought you would, old boy. Just a moment then . . ."

He came trotting back down the stairs.

Polly didn't like the smirk on his face as he directed her to Cecil's sitting room. But it didn't matter. All that mattered was the business at hand.

Cecil stood up as she entered the room. When he saw who she was, the expression on his face almost made her smile in spite of the nature of her errand.

"P-Polly," he stammered, then he recovered. "So good of you to call. Please sit down. I'll get you something to . . ."

"No," Polly said. "Let's not waste time, Cecil. You know why I'm here."

"Yes. Rotten of me, what? But I hadn't expected things to happen so quickly. I'd planned . . ."

"What had you planned, Cecil?" Polly said.

"To break it off more gently. If I had had more time . . ."

"One cannot break off from his lawful wife, Cecil— gently or not," Polly said.

"Oh, so she told you that, too, eh? Too bad."

"What do you propose to do?"

He turned indolently and crossed to the sideboard. From it, he took a decanter and two glasses.

"I asked you a question, Cecil!"

"D'you know, you're devilish pretty, Polly," Cecil said.

Polly stood up. When she spoke her voice was very low.

"Don't trifle with me, Cecil," she said evenly. "And you may put up your brandy. I don't drink with— swine."

"Now really, Polly——"

"What do you propose to do about Kathy?" Polly said.

"Nothing," Cecil said. Then he poured himself a goblet of brandy. "I'm sorry, Polly, but there's nothing I can do . . ."

"Why not?" Polly said.

He walked over to the mantel and picked up a small box of red leather, embossed in gold. He handed it to Polly.

Then she saw that it wasn't a box at all, but three leather-bound frames, hinged so that they folded into that shape. She opened them and looked into the faces of three exquisitely painted miniatures: a dark-haired woman, whose face was soft and gentle and sweet, and two children with faces like cherubs.

"Permit me," Cecil said mockingly, "to present the Lady Agatha, my wife, and Percy and Cecil Second—my sons. . . ."

Polly looked at them a long time. Then she closed the frames back together and stood up.

"They're lovely," she said. "My felicitations, Cecil."

Cecil Fitzgerald stared at her.

"You know," he said, "you're a lady—the first I've ever met in this accursed country . . ."

"Thank you," Polly said. Then she went back down the stairs.

She was surprised at Kathy's reaction when she told her. Kathy didn't appear to hear her. She didn't seem to really understand. When Polly left the room, she made a sound like sobbing. Outside in the hall, Polly heard it. She pushed open the door and went back again. But Kathy wasn't crying. She was laughing.

"Oh, Polly!" she gasped. "It's funny, isn't it? It really is much too funny—the kind of fool I've been. Believing him all this time, living on—hope . . . So funny, so very, very funny—the funniest thing in this whole wide world!"

Polly stared at her. Then she saw the tears on her face. She went over and sat down on the edge of the bed and took her sister in her arms. It wasn't laughter any more.

The two things are very close, aren't they? Polly thought. There's never more than a hairsbreadth between our laughter, and our tears. . . .

She sat there a long time, rocking gently back and forth, cradling her sister in her arms.

It was the whine of the wind that awakened her about two hours before dawn. She lay there listening to it, hearing the sandlike grating of the sleet against the windowpane. She felt cold down to the very marrow of her bones despite the covers.

Poor Kathy, she thought. She must be freezing. I'd better have a look at her.

She got up, put on her robe and slippers, and picked up her candle, sheltering it with one hand against the gusts that shook the house. In Kathy's room, the candle burned fitfully, quivering on its floating saucer. But Kathy wasn't there. The sheets were icy to Polly's touch. Kathy must have been gone for hours.

She had to be calm. She went down and woke up Terrence, and told him to harness the horses to the sleigh. Then she dressed very carefully in her warmest things, putting on her heaviest coat, her furs, her gloves, and her muff. Then she went downstairs, to where Terrence waited with the sleigh.

"Yes," Cecil said, "she's been here. Oh—about eleven,

say. I sent her home in a sleigh. My own man, Rodney, drove her. . . . What's that? She isn't home, yet? Good Lord! Wait a moment, Polly—I'll get dressed and——"

"No, thank you," Polly said. "I'll find her, Cecil."

From their new house, the East River was closer than the Hudson. So Polly, whose mind was working very well and very clearly, drove eastward first. It took her less than ten minutes to find Kathy. She hadn't gotten anywhere near the river. She lay in an open space between two houses, where the wind came through unchecked. She looked like a little mound of snow, there on the sidewalk. When they lifted her up, the tears were frozen on her cheeks, her lashes and brows were ice-crusted. Polly couldn't even get her mouth open to get the brandy down.

Old Dr. Reynolds shook his head.

"It's bad, Polly," he said. "Both hands—and both feet. They'll have to come off. And I don't think she could stand it. She seems to be half starved as well . . ."

"You mean she's going to die, don't you?" Polly whispered.

"Yes, Polly," Dr. Reynolds said.

It took her a long time, though. More than a week. Long enough for Ethan Page to slip into the city, past the drunken Hessian guards, and find the house.

He stood there looking down at her wasted figure, seeing her hands turned black, and her arms, too, almost to the elbows.

"Why, Polly!" he whispered. "Why?"

Polly told him.

He stood there, looking at her.

"Where does he live?" he said.

And Polly told him that, too, because it was no good now to try to keep it back.

"I'll be back in an hour," Ethan said.

Polly sat there, looking at her sister.

You've won, she thought. Even dying, you've won. He's gone to fight Cecil because of you, and I'll have nothing left—either way. Even if he wins, I couldn't have him now—not knowing that he turned to me finally only because you're not there . . .

Something about Kathy attracted her attention. Kathy was still—too still. She leaned over her. Touched one eyelid with her finger. Raised it. Then, very gently, she let it fall.

Then she put down her face against the coverlets and cried.

When Ethan reached the house where Cecil was quartered, there was no sentry there. It was far too cold. The sentry had repaired to a tavern to imbibe some liquid warmth. Ethan sood there, staring at the house. I'm a fool, he thought. Kathy isn't worth it— never was. But she's Polly's sister, and there are no men of that blood. Can't let them debauch our women and go back to brag of it. Got to have it out with him now, if I can find him.

He put his shoulder against the door and pushed. It was bolted. He moved back across the street and crashed into it. But he wasn't strong enough, and it made far too much noise.

He circled the house. On the far side he found a

low window. He put the tip of his saber under it and pried. It came up, quite easily.

He moved through the hall until he came to an open door. He went in, stood there staring at the sleeping figure of a man. He couldn't tell whether the man was Cecil or not. It was too dark for that.

So he put out his hand and shook him gently.

"Eh, what?" the man said.

"Major Fitzgerald?" Ethan said.

"Second floor," the man mumbled. "First room to the right of the stair . . . Can't a chap get any blasted sleep in this place?"

"Thank you," Ethan said. Before he got to the door, the man was snoring.

He shook Cecil awake with less gentleness. He put the saber against his throat.

"Don't make a sound," he said flatly, "or you're dead. Get up and get dressed . . ."

"Who're you?" Cecil croaked.

"Colonel Ethan Page, of the Army of the United States of America," Ethan told him. "Hop to it, now— look alive."

"Might I ask what this is all about?" Cecil said as he drew on his breeches.

"Kathy. I was engaged to her once. She's dying— perhaps dead by now. Your fault, Major. I aim to see that you pay for it."

"I see. So you Americans settle affairs of this sort with murder—eh?"

"No," Ethan said quietly. "I'm taking your saber along, too. When we're far enough from the house not to attract too much attention with the noise, I'll give it back to you. . . ."

Five blocks away from that house, they stood and faced each other in the snow. Cecil Fitzgerald was a fine swordsman, which Ethan was not. But Ethan had Valley Forge inside him, and Morristown, and five hundred bitter retreats. The fury inside his body was like fire, warming him, driving him on.

The blades clashed in the frosty night, showering sparks upon the snow. They hacked at each other for five minutes. Ten. The sweat ran down their backs in rivulets, then froze against their skin.

Cecil moved in, a whirlwind of razor-edged steel whirling about his head. His blade went under Ethan's parry, opened a ten-inch gash along Ethan's left side.

Ethan could feel the strength pumping out of him. He swayed on his feet. The sleet lashed his face, his eyes.

Then Cecil was upon him, beating him down by main force. He felt his feet going out from under him, and the darkness roaring about his head. The stars were blotted out by the swirl of whiteness. It fell into his face, blinding him.

He felt, rather than saw, Cecil moving in to finish him. Then he lashed out with both feet. He caught Cecil full in the chest, sending him over backwards. He dragged himself upright groggily, and thrust out hard. He felt his blade go through cloth, through flesh, something hot and sticky and wet jetted out over his hand.

When he got the sleet out of his eyes, he saw Cecil Fitzgerald bending over his sword, coughing out his life into the snow. It took him a long time to go down. Ethan turned to walk away. He got ten feet down the road before the earth rose up and struck him in the face.

An hour later, Polly stood in that street beside the sleigh that had brought her there, watching Terrence and another servant lifting Ethan into the sleigh. Taking Cecil's address as the starting point she had searched all the nearby streets until she came upon them. She could trust her servants. They were almost like her own flesh and blood. They put him down gently and covered him with blankets. He was bleeding fearfully.

She glanced at Cecil's body, already half covered with snow. God forgive him, she thought, and take care of his little sons. . . .

"Home, Miss Polly?" Terrence said.

"No," Polly said. "Drive down to William Street, Terry. Our old barn's still standing. The redcoats will never think of looking there. And the snow will cover our tracks in ten minutes. Then you go get Doc Reynolds . . ."

"He'll live," Doc Reynolds whispered later. "If he doesn't freeze to death, and if you can get some food in him. He should be in a good warm bed . . ."

Polly looked at Ethan, lying in the straw.

"Don't worry, Doctor," she said, "I'll keep him warm."

Doc Reynolds sewed up the saber slash that Cecil's blade had made along Ethan's left side. It was an ugly-looking wound, but it wasn't particularly dangerous. The trouble was that Ethan Page was so weakened by years of semi-starvation that any kind of wound might prove dangerous to him.

Polly and Doc Reynolds wrapped him up as warmly

as they could and lay him down in the hay. It would have been better to move him to a house and a bed, but they couldn't do that this night. They both knew that the British had found Cecil Fitzgerald's body by now and were searching the streets for the man who had killed him.

They would come to her house first, Polly knew. The young Lieutenant would remember her previous visit. Besides, all the younger officers knew of Cecil's connection with Kathy.

Nothing to do then but to sit here and wait in an icy barn. Walking back and forth to try to keep warm, staring out of the windows at the bleak chimneys that were all that was left of the house you'd lived in as a child. . . .

She heard Ethan groan. She knelt down beside him, touched his face. His body was like ice. He'd lost so much blood that his body couldn't maintain its natural heat; even with all the blankets and the straw, he was freezing.

She couldn't make a fire. There was no place in the barn that a fire could be laid. She couldn't get the brandy down Ethan's throat. Unconscious as he was, it would only strangle him. Ethan was going to die. And she was going to have to sit there and watch him. After having watched Kathy. It was too much. Far too much. She whirled and started toward the ladder. But at the top of it she stopped.

I can't, she thought. I can't leave him. I'd almost forgotten how it was. I'd almost allowed poor John André to bedazzle me. But Ethan's back now and it's the same thing, only worse, like entering again a house you haven't lived in for years and knowing that you're home again in a way that you've never been at home anywhere else. That you've never really been away . . . I can't let him die. Dear God, kind, merciful God, help me to save him. . . .

Whether it was the prayer, or just her simple need that helped, Polly never knew afterward. But there flashed into her mind suddenly the picture of those men in the huts at Valley Forge, huddled together to keep each other warm. She ran over to where Ethan lay, and unwrapped the blankets. Then she lay down close beside him and pulled the blankets over them both. She put her arms around him, and drew him to her, holding him like that until she could feel the chill go out of him and his body growing warm. . . .

It was a simple thing to do, but it filled her with an aching tenderness that was strong and fleshless, and almost maternal. She stroked his poor head, and kissed his dirty, unshaven face, and forgave him a thousand times over for all the pain he'd cost her.

Toward morning, he was in the grip of fever. Polly was asleep, but the sound of his voice awakened her.

"Polly. Been a fool. Been a thundering idiot. Always was Polly, nobody else. Kathy was tinsel, and a grown man can't love tinsel, not really. Blinded by her beauty. Couldn't see her, couldn't see how shallow, fickle, scheming—putting me off when the British came nigh New York, waiting to see who'd win. Made no difference to her. Thumbs up for the redcoats—Cecil. Thumbs up for the bluecoats—me. Fool—bloody fool . . ."

"Hush, Ethan," Polly whispered, "be quiet, my darling . . ."

"Lost Polly now. Price of being a fool. Two letters

since September—written in ice water with a bayonet point for a pen. Had to come back—had to. Come back to Polly. Tell her—make her see . . ."

"Oh, darling," Polly sobbed. "Please, my Ethan, hush!"

"All right. Nothing to be said, anyhow. Lost Polly. Killed my own men. Deserted. Had to come back—had to make Polly see . . ."

"I see," Polly whispered "Yes, Ethan—now I see!"

Four days later, when he was stronger, Dr. Reynolds took him out of the city to a farmhouse near the Harlem Heights, hiding him under blankets and straw in the back of the sleigh. Polly couldn't go with him, because the British were watching her. They had already questioned her twice, trying to find some clue to Cecil's death. She hadn't told them anything, but they weren't satisfied.

The next night, Polly mounted her fastest horse and rode cautiously through the city streets, winding about to disguise her direction until she came to the wooded section north of the city. Then she brought down her crop hard. She almost made it. But just beyond the thickest patch of woodland, two Hessians sprang out of a thicket and seized the bridle.

They stood there, grinning at her.

"A prize, *nicht wahr*, eh Hans?" one of them said. "So pretty in her furs. It to me gives much joy such a one to have taken . . ."

"Speak English," Polly begged. "I have money. I'll pay you . . ."

But the big Hessian put up his hand and took her arm.

"Down with you, my pretty one," he laughed. "Because this night for all the frostbite and hunger in this crazy land I shall rewarded be . . ."

There was no help for it. Polly put her free hand inside her muff. She didn't draw the pistol out. She simply turned the muff edgewise and fired through it. The big Hessian went down, falling into his companion's arms.

And Polly was off again, galloping through the woodland. She didn't stop until she reached the farmhouse where Ethan lay.

It was spring again before Ethan was well enough to walk. Polly had hired a woman to take care of him, and had visited him herself each week end, thanking her stars that her mother and her uncle lingered in Jamaica, where Knowles and Company also had offices dealing in sugar and rum, and where the weather was warm. But when Ethan was finally up and about again, Dr. Reynolds came with her to see him. And with him, the good doctor brought a Congregational minister.

Polly had been reared in the Episcopal faith, but that didn't matter now. As she took Ethan's arm and stood before the kindly little minister with old Doc Reynolds and the farm couple behind her, the words from the Book of Ruth ran through her mind:

". . . . whither thou goest, I will go . . . Where thou diest, will I die, and there will I be buried . . . thy people shall be my people, and thy God, my God . . ."

The next night, the two of them were in a rowboat, on the Hudson, headed once more for New Jersey, and war.

Polly sat very still in the boat, and stared out over the moonwashed waters. Her lips moved, forming words, but she spoke so low that Ethan couldn't hear them.

"What are you saying, my dearest?" he asked her.

"Something very old," Polly answered, "but very beautiful. It's from the Bible—the Book of Ruth:

'. . .whither thou goest, I will go . . . where thou liest, I will lie . . . Where thou diest, will I die; and there will I be buried . . . thy people shall be my people, and thy God, my God . . .' "

Ethan stared at her, and his eyes were very tender in the moonlight.

CHAPTER 9

Polly stood outside the ragged tent she shared with Ethan, holding her arms against her thin body. It did no good. The rain was like needles of ice. She was soaked to the skin. But she didn't move. Polly Page, Mistress Ethan Page, stood there in the driving rain because she could not sleep.

When the guns started at last, she could hear them. It was almost a relief when the sound came over to her, rolling through the rain.

It was the night of October ninth, 1781. And the guns of Colonel d'Avoville, slow-rolling, bass-voiced, belly-deep, were pounding a place called Yorktown.

Now, Polly thought, now. This will be the last time. After this he will be safe . . . I can't stand any more.

She could see the rockets rising in red arcs, hissing through the rain. She stood there, shivering, hugging her tattered shawl to her for warmth. But only her body was conscious of the cold. Her mind wasn't there. It was out in front, where a line of men in patched, ragged clothes, and now—thank God—boots borrowed from the French, stood knee-deep in the flooded trenches, waiting the signal to attack.

She knew when the signal came, because the big guns stopped. She stood there, clenching and unclenching her hands.

After all these years, God, You couldn't let him
. . . she prayed.

It took ten days. The Soissonnais, the Auvergnats, and
all the other French troops fought like inspired demons. Never again could the Americans make jokes
about "dainty Frog-eaters." As for the Americans,
themselves, they were demons—demons, madmen,
fiends from hell.

And at two o'clock in the afternoon of Friday, October 19, 1781, the British Army under Lord Cornwallis surrendered.

Polly saw it. They came marching out over the
Hampton Road to the tune of drums and fifes playing,
"The World Turned Upside Down." Cornwallis
couldn't go through with it. He sent General O'Hara
to surrender in his name. O'Hara tried to surrender to
Rochambeau; but the Comte Dumas wouldn't permit
that. He sent him to George Washington, instead.

And Washington, who was always magnificent at
the right time, refused Cornwallis' sword, saying:

"Never from so good a hand!"

Watching it, Polly was crying, without knowing why
she cried. The redcoats and the bluecoated Hessians
marched by, laying their flags down, stacking their
arms. They weren't an army any more. They were
prisoners of war.

And the Americans and the French fell into marching formation. The bands struck up an old tune—
the finest, Polly thought, the greatest, the sweetest
tune in the world:

> Yankee Doodle, keep it up,
> Yankee Doodle, Dandy,

Mind the music, and the step,
And with the girls be handy!

She raced back to camp. She was there when he came, getting awkwardly, tiredly down from his bony nag, limping as he came towards her in that blessed silence of no more guns. He was weary, gaunt, gray. His uniform was faded, patched. But as she put out her arms and flew to him, Polly Page didn't care about those things.

He was safe. That was all that mattered. And nothing in all the years ahead would ever keep him from her. . . .

if you enjoy
GOOD FICTION

THESE GREAT BEST SELLERS NOW AVAILABLE IN INEXPENSIVE PAPERBACKS ORDER THEM HERE!

THE DARK RIVER by Nordoff & Hall R-998 50¢
The authors of Mutiny On The Bounty weave an enchanting story of love and adventure in the South Seas. First time in paperback.

THE GREAT SNOW by Henry Morton Robinson R-978 50¢
The revealing story of husbands, wives and lovers told with genuine gusto . . . by the author of The Cardinal.

THE GREEN BAY TREE by Louis Bromfield X-968 50¢
Bromfield's classic—an unforgettable portrayal of human passions, ranging from America to Paris, spanning two decades between two wars.

WITHOUT ARMOR by James Hilton R-956 50¢
An incredible adventure—and a love story—set against the flaming backdrop of the Russian Revolution.

THE OFFICER FACTORY by Hans Hellmut Kirst T-954 75¢
An infamous officers' training camp turns men into brutes and makes women their wanton partners.

CASTLE GARAC by Nicholas Monsarrat R-943 50¢
In the finest tradition of Daphne du Maurier . . . suspense, romance and intrigue in a French castle.

THE HURRICANE by Nordoff & Hall R-928 50¢
The popular South Seas adventure saga by the authors of The Dark River and Mutiny On The Bounty.

DYNASTY OF DEATH by Taylor Caldwell N-891 95¢
A famous author's most famous novel in its first paperback unabridged edition.

CLAUDIA by Rose Franken R-798 50¢
Two novels in one. The wonderful marriage of Claudia and David Naughton—their early years, triumphs and tragedies.

NOTE: Pyramid pays postage on orders for four books or more. On orders for less than four books, add 10¢ per book to cover postage and handling.

————— WHEREVER PAPERBACKS ARE SOLD OR USE THIS COUPON. —————

PYRAMID BOOKS, Dep't. K-102, 444 Madison Ave., New York, N.Y. 10022

Please send the best-sellers circled below. I enclose $_____.
R-998 R-978 X-968 R-956 T-954 R-943 R-928 N-891 R-893 R-798

Name_____

Street Address_____

City_____ State_____

**PYRAMID
BOOKS**